Warsaw Stories

BY HERSH DOVID NOMBERG

Translated by Daniel Kennedy

Introduction and Translator's Notes
by Daniel Kennedy

White Goat Press
A Yiddish Book Center Translation

Amherst, Massachusetts
yiddishbookcenter.org

This publication was made possible with the generous support of

The Applebaum Foundation

With additional funding from
Della Peretti
The Wortman Family

Yiddish Book Center
Amherst, MA 01002

978-0-9893731-9-7

Special first printing for the Yiddish Book Center's *Great Jewish Books Book Club*.

Cover photograph from the Archives of the YIVO Institute for Jewish Research, New York
Book and cover design by Michael Grinley

"The Golden Fantasy" was originally published in *Storgy*, June 2016
"Letters" was originally published in the *2016 Pakn Treger Digital Translation Issue*
"Gossip" was originally published in *Pakn Treger* (Issue 74, 2016)

Contents

Introduction

In 1897, at the age of twenty-one, Hersh Dovid Nomberg arrived in Warsaw to seek his fortune as a writer.

At the time Warsaw was experiencing a period of intense growth. Between the mid-nineteenth century and the outbreak of the first world war, the city had almost quadrupled in size, going from being the seventeenth largest city in Europe to the eighth largest. It was a city of multistory buildings, bustling crowded streets, and horse-drawn tramlines. There were rail connections to Vienna and St. Petersburg and even an extensive underground sewage system.[1] The first power plant was built in 1904 and electric streetlights were installed in 1907 followed by the first electric tramline a year later. The demographic composition of the city remained remarkably stable, despite the massive influx of new residents: In 1897 the city was roughly 34 percent Jewish,[2] 56 percent Polish, and 7 percent Russian (not counting the military garrison).

Since 1867 what had once been the Kingdom of Poland[3] was now "Vistula Land," a fully-fledged part of the Russian Empire. A process of forced Russification in the later half of the nineteenth century culminated in a complete ban on the use of Polish in education and in all public institutions.

---

[1] Though most landlords were unwilling to pay to have their properties connected to the system, leaving the majority of tenants without indoor plumbing.

[2] Ten percent of whom spoke Polish at home.

[3] Informally known as Congress Poland, originally a sovereign state connected by personal union with Russia, during the 19th century it was gradually stripped of autonomy and integrated into the Russian Empire.

The Russian Empire was by all accounts a deeply repressive, autocratic state. Freedom of expression and free association simply did not exist; police approval was needed (and generally declined) for all public gatherings of more than a dozen people; political parties were effectively illegal; books, newspapers, and periodicals were subject to censorship; passports were required to move from one part of the country to another (Jews being confined to an area in the west known as the Pale of Settlement); there was an extensive system of police surveillance; and justice could be severe and arbitrary. The period of 1904–1907 in particular was one of significant political unrest in the Empire. Beginning with the Russo-Japanese war and culminating in the ultimately failed revolution of 1905, it was a time of economic instability, riots, work stopagges, anti-Jewish pogroms, and political assassinations.

Nomberg came to Warsaw from the small town of Ashminov (Mszczonów in Polish), where he had been raised in a strictly religious Hasidic environment by his maternal grandfather, Nomberg's father having died young. As a child, Nomberg contracted tuberculosis and was sent to recover in a sanitorium in Otwock, fourteen miles from Warsaw. He survived but would suffer from chronic health problems for much of his life. He married at eighteen and lived with his new in-laws *af kest:* a traditional arrangement whereby room and board is provided by the bride's parents in order to allow a young groom to continue his religious studies. Nomberg however did not continue his religious studies; instead he began teaching himself Polish, Russian, and German, and experienced a crisis of faith. Nomberg's newfound atheism and growing literary ambitions were intolerable to his in-laws, and he was forced to separate from his wife and two infant sons, compounding his already melancholic state.

Upon arrival in Warsaw, his first impulse was to meet with preeminent Jewish writer I. L. Peretz, whose Hebrew poetry had left a deep impression on him. Peretz did as he always did when visited by young Jewish writers from the provinces: he praised Nomberg's poems, advised him to try writing in Yiddish, and welcomed him into his literary circle.

Nomberg began publishing short stories, poems, translations, journalism, and literary criticism, both in Hebrew and in Yiddish, in various newspapers. His literary breakthrough came with the short story "Fliglman," an instant success, which left a lasting mark on Yiddish and Hebrew literature alike. "Fliglman" is a finely drawn study of a character whose name became a byword for the type of young men who came to the cities to live new lives as intellectuals, philosophers, teachers, and artists, cut off from tradition, estranged from their community, while remaining unable to assimilate fully into modern Europe. As Abraham Suhl notes:

> Everyone instantly recognises Fliglman. Often in his own breast. The streets are teeming with Fliglmans. Nomberg depicts him with apparent objectivity, yet he secretly detests him with a contemptuous irony, for he himself is also a Fliglman.[4]

Peretz's literary circle soon expanded to include other young writers such as Sholem Asch and Avrom Reyzen, both of whom shared an apartment with Nomberg for a time. Reyzen notes that, even in those early days, Nomberg began mentoring and encouraging his fellow writers:

> His critiques were strict, often mercilessly so, but in those days he had a powerful influence over me.[5]

While their mentor Peretz kept his day job and was often reluctant to accept payment for his own stories, Nomberg had ambitions of transforming the business of being a Jewish writer into a bona fide

---

4 Abraham Suhl, preface to *Flügelmann: Novellen aus dem Jüdischen* (Leipzig: Schemesch Verlag, 1924), vii.

5 Avrom Reyzen, *Epizodn fun mayn lebn* (Vilna: Vilber farlag fun B. Kletskin, 1929), 211.

profession. Nomberg even confronted Peretz on Avrom Reyzen's behalf, insisting that Reyzen receive an honorarium for the poems that
he had published in Peretz's journal, *Kultur-bleter*. As Nomberg saw it,
the press was the only means of achieving his goal:

> The logic is simple: Jews read newspapers, not books . . . they
> know that a newspaper costs money and are willing to pay for
> it—and when they do happen to read a book, they somehow
> feel as though they should be the ones getting paid.[6]

By 1904 Nomberg was editor-in-chief of *Ha-Tsofeh*, the second
of Warsaw's two Hebrew-language daily newspapers, and in 1905 he
joined the staff of *Der veg*, a new Yiddish-language daily. He left Warsaw briefly to travel abroad, spending time in Germany, France, and
Switzerland. In 1907 he returned to Warsaw, only to leave again for
Riga, where he co-founded the *Natsyonaler-tsaytung*, Riga's first Yiddish-language newspaper. He spent time in Vilna, where he worked
for various newspapers, and established links between Warsaw and
Vilna's literary circles, publishing an anthology of writings from the
two cities.

Nomberg was a short, thin man with a disproportionately large head
and piercing blue eyes. Ever restless and full of energy, he was a com-
pulsive socialite, always dragging people to cafés, staying out every
night until dawn, and sleeping during the day.

Despite having made Warsaw his home, Nomberg was, as Froyim
Kaganovski put it, always running away. He preferred to stay in
hotels rather than settle at any one address. He obsessively collected
gadgets—cameras, newfangled shaving devices, and strange tooth-
brushes—which he brought back from his frequent trips abroad,
along with stockpiles of ground Turkish coffee.

The years 1901–1907 marked the highpoint of Nomberg's literary
phase, and all the stories in this volume come from that time. Afterward,

---

[6] Quoted in Froyim Kaganovski, *Yidishe shrayber in der heym* (Paris: Farlag afsnay, 1956), 373.

while never giving up writing fiction entirely, Nomberg increasingly concentrated his energies on journalism and a wide range of cultural undertakings.

In 1908 Nomberg attended the Czernowitz language conference, and is credited with drafting the famous compromise resolution proclaiming Yiddish as *a* national language of the Jewish people, rather than *the* national language.

During the First World War, when Warsaw was occupied by German troops, he became involved in the secular Yiddish school movement and was one of the founding members of the Union of Jewish Writers and Journalists, whose address at Tłomackie 13 became the new center for Jewish literary life in the city in the period after Peretz's death.[7]

Following Polish independence Nomberg briefly dabbled in politics, serving as a delegate to the Sejm in 1921, representing the *Folkspartey*, a party dedicated to safeguarding secular Jewish cultural autonomy within the Polish Republic. In the twenties he traveled extensively, visiting the United States, Argentina, the Soviet Union, and Palestine.

Nomberg's health gradually deteriorated until one night in 1927, while leaving the Writers' Union at Tłomackie 13, he collapsed on the stairs. He was taken to a sanitorium in Otwock where he later died, at the age of fifty-one.

---

7 During the Tłomackie 13 years Nomberg developed an obsession for dancing, particularly the tango; he provided the Union with a gramophone and it soon became a venue for late-night social gatherings.

Warsaw Stories

Fliglman

Who and What Is Fliglman & Concerning His Acquaintances

Fliglman was a young man in his early thirties. He had a small, somewhat crooked body, a large, lopsided forehead, and a little blond beard. His eyes looked like they were fogged up with steam, as if all one needed to do was wipe them with a handkerchief for them to shine brightly.

Often, as he ambled through the busy streets on his way to a lesson, hunched up, hands in pockets, he thought about how many great men had lived in the world: Buddha, Spinoza, Kant, and many others, and he, the son of a lowly shammes from Kuniv, knew their philosophical systems inside out and could recite everything they had ever written word for word.

And if the sun happened to be shining, the carriages weren't clamoring in his ears, and he wasn't in any particular hurry to get to his lesson, then he would savor the thought that, deep down, all those philosophers were not especially clever—each one had hidden himself away in his own little corner and uncovered a piece of the great puzzle, but only a small piece, while he, Fliglman, knew everything they had achieved; what's more he knew that the main thing, the kernel of everything, was life! Life itself was the thing!

And Fliglman was satisfied with his life. The first five years in Warsaw had not been easy, and he preferred not to dwell on those days; back then he had been a man without firm convictions, without a *Weltanschauung*, as he called it. But over the past eight years he had managed to settle himself in, find some work as a private tutor, and he had started to lead a peaceful life based on a few strict principles, living somewhat removed from the world in his room high up on the fifth floor.

His room was always set up in a special way: Fliglman's way. He refused the services of a maid, being vehemently against slavery in all its forms. But when it came to washing the floor, which he couldn't do on his own, he would end up having to make compromises and reproach himself. How difficult it was to exist in this world while remaining a respectable person!

He had many acquaintances but few close friends. In his circle he was considered well educated, a philosopher and an aesthete, but his name did not come up often in conversation. Whole months could go by without anyone thinking about him. They would only remember him when money was needed, and then someone would cry: "We forgot all about Fliglman!"

"So we did!" another would say, and they would all wonder how Fliglman could have completely slipped their minds.

When he had guests, Fliglman would welcome them with tea, inquire after mutual acquaintances, lend money; but he avoided getting into debates for the sake of it and made sure the conversation did not become too intimate, so as not to contaminate his *Weltanschauung*. The acquaintance would leave satisfied, telling all his friends. In this way, everyone sang Fliglman's praises, but he was soon forgotten again for another couple of months.

His closest friend was Levantkovski: teacher, father of six, a poor man but a happy one. They had met in a bookshop. Levantkovski had a peculiar relationship to books. Whenever there was a new book out in Hebrew or Yiddish that Levantkovski was not able to buy immediately, he would become depressed and agitated; sitting in Fliglman's room he could not bring himself to drink his tea. Fliglman often lent him money to buy books, provoking the ire of Levantkovski's wife, who reprimanded him for lending Levantkovski so much money.

Fliglman liked to confide in Levantkovski and often talked about himself:

"The poets believe that they alone feel the beauty of nature. This is false! The only difference between the poets and myself is that they know how to express their feelings in poetic form, and I don't. That's not my concern. Take for example the fact that I pay an extra ruble for my room just because the moon shines in at night. I'm an honest man; I arranged it like that with the landlady: I pay an extra ruble every month with the sole condition that there be moonlight in the room. You know, Levantkovski, the masses, the simple people, can sometimes be crude. Try to picture the smile on my landlady's face when I asked her if the moon shines into the room at night! You understand? She took me for an imbecile . . . To cut a long story short, I tell you, Levantkovski, it's hard to live in this world as a decent, intelligent person. Yes indeed!"

Fliglman was speaking in Russian, and even though Levantkovski had trouble understanding the difficult words, he nodded in agreement and proceeded to read Fliglman a poem he had written about nature.

"It's a good poem," said Fliglman. "It just needs a deeper philosophical perspective. For example, you say: 'Oh how nature is idyllic, every mountain, every hillock.' Yet a true poet feels that the mountains and the heavens and the earth—all of nature—are one and the same as we ourselves . . ."

"What do you mean?" asked Levantkovski, his face turning deadly serious as though he were about to cry. His gaping mouth revealed two long rows of teeth, and his hand trembled in midair.

"Take me, for example; I feel it quite clearly. I often have the impression that I am part of the sky and the moon and everything else, that we are all the same thing, all one absolute, you understand? Just in different forms . . ."

"Listen to that—in different forms! But that's exactly what I said! What do you want, honestly!"

And Levantkovski flailed his hand around until Fliglman's good mood turned sour; he hated when people got worked up.

"Anyway, the poem is good," he said. "We'll talk about it again another time. Good night."

Levantkovski's wife, an old woman with a yellowish face and sunken breasts, followed Fliglman, as she often did, and stopped him:

"Panie Fliglman, you wouldn't be able to spare fifty kopeks by any chance?"

Fliglman handed her the money and lingered in the hall a while. He soon heard a heated argument between husband and wife: Levantkovski wanted fifteen kopeks to buy tobacco, but his wife did not want to give it to him, so he rebuked her that if it weren't for him, Fliglman wouldn't have lent her the money in the first place, and she said: "You're not worthy of even speaking to him!"

Levantkovski fell silent, and Fliglman could hear him pacing around his apartment. A contented smile appeared on Fliglman's face, where it remained until he arrived home and sat down to read.

He read for a long time, slowly and always in the same pose: sitting with a calm, earnest expression on his face. If he came to a noteworthy passage, he would pause and read it through a second time, thereby memorizing it. Then, giving his mustache a tug, he would resume reading, and it seemed as though his brain never tired of devouring page after page, just as his lungs never tired of air. As time passed, he would take out his watch, and if it was already eleven he would close the book and give his mustache another tug as a strange sweetness spread over his face.

And if the moon was in the patch of sky that was visible through the window, he would put out the lamp, move his chair up close to the window, and look at the moon. He smoked a cigarette, pulling on it slowly. The smoke curled in the blue-tinged air and the moon swam in the fog, slow, pious, and earnest. Fliglman hummed an old Hasidic melody to himself—the only tune that his ears had ever managed to catch. The fog began to clear, and the moon rose higher, together with the dark sky. Fliglman held his head up high, gazing long and hard, and had the impression that he, the sky, the moon, and the whole world were one and the same thing—one absolute in different forms—and that life was everything. Afterward, lying on his bed, he would drift off to sleep with the thought that an intellectual life was not only the most honest but also the best and most beautiful, and that, in addition, his own life was rich in poetry.

That's the kind of man that Fliglman was.

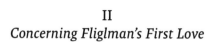

II
Concerning Fliglman's First Love

Fliglman held love in very high regard.

"Love," he would say, "is the main principle of life. Life without love has no meaning and loses all justification. A person who is not inclined to love by nature has less value than one who cannot read or write."

Fliglman himself was by nature very inclined to love. But if one lives a life of reason and intellect, one must be prepared to live in isolation and solitude.

"I cannot tell lies; I cannot flatter," he would say to comfort himself for his awkwardness with women. And he always hoped he would one day encounter a soul that could feel his own soul, because, frankly speaking, no shallow soul would ever be capable of loving him.

One time—having just moved into a new apartment—he noticed, in a window on the opposite side of the street, a pale figure with black hair, wearing a light-colored blouse with a stiff collar as white as snow. Her eyes were large and dark and she was looking directly over at Fliglman's window.

It was early in the morning and bright outside; one half of the wall opposite was bathed in sunlight. The windows were open and the girl, shielding her eyes from the sun, looked in his direction. Fliglman looked too. The girl lowered her gaze, ashamed. Her chest rose and fell as though with a sigh. Enthralled, Fliglman continued to observe her. But the girl looked up once again before turning away in embarrassment. Her chest heaved again. Fliglman tapped on the window pane with two fingers and said to himself: "Enough!"

He stepped away from the window, satisfied that he had

restrained himself by not continuing to stare, although he had very much wanted to.

"A man's greatest triumph is to conquer himself," he thought afterward, walking down the street to his next lesson. But during the lesson he felt strangely restless; he felt something moving inside him, near his heart, something creeping up at regular intervals and taking a bite, then retreating. The black hair and light blouse with the white collar lingered in his mind's eye, and he was in good spirits, almost giddy, as he used to be back in the old days, just before Passover.

"Hmmm . . . yes!" he thought to himself throughout the day, wiping his mustache, barely uttering another word, as though hiding some secret from himself. A smile lay on his face all day long.

In bed that night, he had barely closed his eyes when the bed turned and he found himself facing the window. He was still thinking about the figure he had seen that morning, and against the black backdrop of night he perceived many tiny points of fire, along with something white trailing out behind them like a light fog. As they floated, the points of light seemed to form a straight geometric line between his window and the one opposite. Just then he remembered that he was in bed. He tried to reorient himself, but when he touched the wall and opened his eyes the bed had moved again, and he found himself looking straight at his white stove. He sat up and looked around. It was dark in the building opposite. He lay back down, and a few minutes later the bed was once again facing the wrong way.

"Hmm," he mumbled, smiling to himself, and drifted off into a fresh dream.

The next morning the girl was at the window again. She was reading a book, so now Fliglman was able to watch her as long as he wanted, but without warning the girl looked up and gazed at Fliglman, directly at him, and there was something in her expression.

"A person's soul is reflected in the eyes, and in laughter," Fligman said to himself, repeating a phrase from some book he'd read long ago. "Remarkable how well phrased that is."

He went over to his little mirror, took a good long look at his face, and found that his gaze and that of the girl were exactly the same. There could be no doubt about it: she liked him. "One soul feels another."

It went on like this for two weeks. The girl would sit by the window while Fliglman watched. Once, as he was observing her, she looked up suddenly as usual, only this time instead of looking away she stared proudly into his eyes, holding his gaze so long that he, Fliglman, was the one who looked away in shame! Later, when he stole another peek at her, she was smiling and her chest bobbed freely. Fliglman felt that he had been conquered by a girl.

"A strong folk," he said that same day, talking with Levantkovski, as they sat in Fliglman's room drinking tea, "those women are a strong folk . . ."

"Oho!" Levantkovski answered, and started telling a story about his wife.

"Wait, Levantkovski, please, you're misunderstanding me. That's not where I'm coming from. I'm talking about how when there's an argument they speak with so much more tact and assurance than men do, because they're secure in their power, in their beauty; actually beauty is everything. After all, aesthetics is the highest *Weltanshauung*, plainly speaking."

As he usually did when his friend began one of his lofty speeches, Levantkovski held his tongue, poured himself some more tea, and put on a serious expression, like a child being scolded by a grandfather. Every now and then he would look at Fliglman and let out a sigh before resuming his earnest pose. Fliglman continued:

"Truth be told, we know nothing. The strands of the psyche are so bewilderingly tangled that it's easy to become a mystic. For example: you meet someone on the street, let's say a girl. You look at her, she looks at you, and a kind of struggle takes place between the two gazes; they do battle with each other, and one is victorious . . . how does this happen? That's where spiritualism begins. But, you understand, pure reason demands that we look for an interpretation, we must connect everything within the law of causality, placing question marks wherever there is a doubt and refusing to accept the mystery . . . I know for certain from my own experience that if it weren't for my faculty of reason I would have long ago become a mystic. Yes indeed!"

"You're certainly very well read," sighed Levantkovski.

"Reading is not what's important," Fliglman said, becoming very serious. "You understand, philosophy seeks to construct life out of theories, but life is much, much broader—in practice, one needs to seek the truth . . . Try to comprehend what I'm saying, think about it."

That night the moon shone round and pure. It popped out from behind a chimney on the rooftop opposite. Thin, low clouds made their way across the sky, and the moon ran between them, ran and yet stayed in the same place. In the courtyard everything was bathed in a bluish air. In the building across the way a light still burned behind closed shutters, and so Fliglman sat by his window, looking from the sky to the window and back again.

The shutters opened and a familiar head looked out. The arms—two naked arms of a young woman—stretched. Her hair was in disarray . . . And Fliglman's gaze shot back toward the moon.

"A crafty folk," he thought, and went to sleep in a state of agitation.

One evening, Fliglman was reading a book. The rain fell heavily—a storm. Thunder boomed with such force that after each thunderclap Fliglman ran toward the window to make sure that everything was still intact, and he saw that across the way the girl was looking out.

She did not appear to notice him. She sat with her chin propped on her hands, her frightened eyes watching the black clouds, and there was a sadness in those eyes that far outweighed the clouds overhead.

Fliglman paced impatiently around his room.

The storm came to an end and the sun came out. Everything was fresh and clean. Fliglman stood by the window and stared. The girl also looked up several times with a bold gaze. A little timidly at first, but growing ever more audacious, Fliglman stared with determination, and his face prepared to smile. The girl glanced up again and then vanished without warning, only to come back several times, apparently quite agitated.

"It's the right moment," thought Fliglman, gathering his courage. He nodded, and a tender smile spread over his face. But the girl stood up abruptly, and the last thing Fliglman saw before the shutters slammed shut was the girl's big red tongue sticking out at him.

It took a moment for Fliglman to regain his composure. He saw that the shutters were closed, and at that exact moment a rainbow appeared.

Lying in bed that night, he bit his lips hard and could not find the right words to express the feeling he carried in his heart: contempt or anger? Points of light again floated in the darkness as they had the other night, only now they drifted without any order at all, spreading in every direction, until the only thing left before his eyes was the blackness. Before he could fall asleep, the bed turned and spiraled in an empty void.

He awoke certain that he must strengthen his resolve to fight against unhappiness, that a reasonable, intelligent person should never let his mood slump. Speaking with Levantkovski he said:

"Care is needed. One must constantly build up one's strength to prepare for any misfortune. I can tell you that if I weren't prepared for every unexpected eventuality, it would be bad, you understand me, Levantkovski? It would be very bad indeed!"

———•———

III
Concerning Fliglman's Weakened Nerves, His Desire to Marry & How He Went Mad

Two years passed, and little had changed in Fliglman's life. Only the longing in his heart for a wife had grown stronger; a longing that often left him shaken, lately making him so anxious that it distracted him from his reading. It happened that he would forget very simple, familiar words, and he often felt dizzy, everything somehow becoming unscrewed and insubstantial.

He was often reminded of his childhood and of his father, a small, thin Jew who was always coughing. On one cold night in particular, his father had crawled out of bed, coughing. Left alone in bed, Fliglman had felt very cold. Then he recalled his father's death: lying there on the ground, he had looked so small that it seemed as if he had curled up and fallen asleep. Fliglman remembered his elder sister crying bitterly, wiping her nose on her apron. They had come to blows on the way home from the funeral, fighting over half an orange that had been lying on the windowsill. After that, Fliglman went off to yeshiva. His sister became a schoolteacher and no longer even tolerated his name to be mentioned, on account of him being an apostate. Naturally, she had many children who went around in rags and were as scruffy and scrawny as Levantkovski's children, while he, Fliglman, was their uncle. Strange how it had all turned out.

His new passport, which Fliglman received from his hometown, stated that he was thirty-six years old. Turning the document over in his hands, Fliglman became pensive. He was distressed by the thought that he had put off marriage for so long. He started to seek out new companionship, but it was not easy for him.

He had recently made the acquaintance of a young woman, a dentist. She was not especially pretty—somewhat plump, with a full face—her laugh was so loud it was difficult to make out what she was saying, and she was fond of constantly braiding and unbraiding her hair. Fliglman began to visit her more and more often, and a hope grew in his heart.

He always talked to her about books, writers, and philosophers. She sat and listened to everything attentively, only interrupting to ask, "Would you like some tea?"

It lasted a whole month.

One time, she went into the other room to make tea, leaving Fliglman alone. He looked around the room, at loose ends. He picked up a small mirror and turned it to face him just as she came in with the tea.

"Having a look at yourself in the mirror too, eh? And you men like to accuse us women of being vain! Honestly, it's laughable!"

"Yes," Fliglman said, drawing out the words, "we men also want to be attractive. It's no great secret. I, for example, would very much like to please *you*."

These last words he uttered softly, in an unsure voice. The woman just asked somewhat bewildered, "Really?" and went quiet.

Fliglman didn't respond. The atmosphere had become tense. The woman opened a book while he stared at the stove.

"How much would a stove like that cost, I wonder—a lovely stove." He spoke in a low voice, and, feeling that he was talking nonsense, he shrugged his shoulders.

She sat in silence for a long time, the book open in front of her, and then she suddenly started to laugh.

"Pathetic, pathetic," she said, pointing to the book, before closing it. Fliglman wasn't sure if she was laughing at him or if there was something funny in the book.

The atmosphere in the room remained heavy and oppressive.

Just then, an acquaintance arrived and the woman's mood brightened. Fliglman stood up to leave, and he never went back to see her again.

One day passed quickly after another. Fliglman lived his lonely life and his nerves grew more and more unsettled. His passport now stated that he was thirty-eight.

A wet and windy autumn came, aggravating Fliglman's condition. While buying a pair of galoshes he forgot his shoe size, mistakenly buying a size too big. Walking through the streets he was unable to forget his error for a single minute: the galoshes kept slipping from his feet, exasperating him.

He had taken to wandering the streets without any particular destination, and had practically given up on reading entirely. The pavement was always wet, and the carriages splashed through the mud; funeral processions passed, both Jewish and Christian. Girls would walk by with books under their arms, holding up their dresses—their white petticoats spattered with mud—as they hurried along. In the evening a porter with a rope for a belt stood on the pavement, swearing that he hadn't earned a single groschen all day.

Fliglman was tired; his brain seemed to be watered down. He felt dizzy and his back ached. He went to see a doctor, who examined him thoroughly and asked if he was married. Fliglman said yes. Afterward it bothered him greatly that he had lied.

"I feel," he said to Levantkovski, "that I'm becoming a pessimist. Actually, pessimism is the last word in philosophy . . ."

He quoted something from Schopenhauer, but as he was speaking he happened to glance at Levantkovski, who sat there slowly rolling a cigarette, trying to stuff in as much tobacco as he could. This disturbed Fliglman, but what annoyed him more was that Levantkovski didn't even seem to notice that he had broken off mid-sentence.

"You know what, Levantkovski?" he suddenly snapped. "You're an idiot!"

Levantkovski paid no attention; he calmly pulled on his cigarette and let out a thick cloud of smoke. Fliglman glared at him long and hard.

"Frankly speaking, what do you need so many children for, Levantkovski? It's really quite irresponsible of you."

Levantkovski smiled.

"So far I have six children; you have none. It's no problem. Let's just say we have three each, how about that? What do you say?"

Levantkovski was pleased with his little joke. He laughed, and his laughter irritated Fliglman even more.

"Listen to me, Levantkovski, you're an idiot, an idiot I tell you. You hear what I'm saying? An idiot . . ." Feeling his temper rise, Fliglman trailed off. Levantkovski's face turned sour. The incident left him baffled, so he said goodbye and exited with his head hung low.

Fliglman was left alone. He started musing over the idea of pessimism, but his thoughts began to dissolve, and he could not remember a passage he had once known by heart. He paced around the apartment saying to himself: "He's an idiot, a complete idiot . . . an idiot . . . an idiot . . . an idiot . . ." For some reason he felt compelled to repeat that same word over and over.

He was terribly shaken for several days. At night, he and his bed sank into a deep abyss. He sighed heavily in his sleep. The weather was so bad that he tried to stay at home as much as he could. Someone in his building had died, and there were mourners crying bitterly in the courtyard, wailing until the black wagon came and carried away the corpse. The courtyard became still.

He tried to read but soon stopped, yawned, and felt lightheaded. He lay down and immediately fell asleep. He had a nightmare. In his dream he was carrying a long, stiff, corpse wrapped up in a black blanket. He clutched the blanket with both hands, hunched over as he walked. He walked from the outskirts of the city in order to bury the body. It was dark. He was accompanied by two shammosim, chatting together. From their conversation he could tell that he was carrying his dead sister. He was exhausted. At the threshold of a shop he slipped, the body fell headfirst onto the stone, and a cry rang out from the blanket, with a voice like a child squealing. One shammes said:

"Carry her, Fliglman, she's dead; it's just an involuntary reflex, carry her!"

He continued carrying the body. The voice trembled more and more, and he felt tired, very tired. The shammosim gave him a push, patted him on the back, and hurried him onward, trying to get him to walk faster. Fliglman felt like crying, but he feared that this might just be an involuntary reflex and that he was in fact already dead. He felt nauseous and got up out of bed with a sigh. A terrible pain spread across his head and back.

The room was so dark that even the sky, covered over with black clouds, let in a clear shine, and this shine was even worse than the darkness. A cat yowled in the courtyard, stopping and then starting again. Its cries cut straight to the heart, and it was impossible to understand what was wrong with the cat, why it was wailing in the darkness so late. Fliglman wrapped himself up in his blanket, while the cat went on yowling. Fliglman did not sleep a wink that night.

During his lesson the next morning he lost his temper with a student. Instead of translating, "The green lamps of your neighbors," the student had said, "The lamps of your green neighbors." Fliglman tried to correct him, but the student repeated: "The lamps of your green neighbors." Fliglman became so enraged he grabbed the student by the shoulders and shook him violently, screaming in a faltering voice: "Green neighbors! How can it be green neighbors? How can that be?"

Suddenly he remembered himself and tried to speak more softly: "Well, tell me, is that possible? How?"

But his voice trembled and his heart pounded; he was breathing heavily and the boy burst into tears.

"Understand! Understand? It's not possible . . ."

The boy ran into the next room, crying to his mother. When the woman looked in, Fliglman felt that he had to make her understand that "green neighbors" was impossible, but he didn't know how to do it. The mother asked: "What happened between you two?"

Fliglman remained silent, but the mother stood and waited. He finally uttered: "Nothing. I'm just a bit rattled today; my sister died."

When the boy's mother became curious about his sister, Fliglman began telling lies—falsehoods that entered his head from who knew where. On his way out he repeated, "I'm sick, I'm sick," and by repeating the word he felt relieved: "sick, sick, sick . . ."

He skipped his other lessons. When he came home in the evening, the sight of his room filled him with dread. He lay down on the bed and fell asleep.

He awoke a while later, gasping for breath and covered in sweat. The room was dark. Startled by a white hand towel, he threw on his coat and began wandering aimlessly until he found himself at Levantkovski's place.

Levantkovski shook his hand with such vigor that something came loose in Fliglman's brain. The room was full of bedding and children's faces. In one bed Levantkovski's wife sighed. Fliglman sat down on a chair and dozed off. He felt Levantkovski's hand; he opened his eyes and saw Levantkovski standing over him, half undressed, smiling.

He said something about being drunk. Levantkovski's smile bothered him, and he wanted to say something stern to wipe the smile from his face.

"I'm going to the Vistula . . ." he just about managed to utter.

"Go back to sleep, it's cold . . ."

Fliglman was indeed struck by how cold it was; the room was fogged up with vapor. Levantkovski smiled and Fliglman got up to leave.

He walked endlessly, only paying attention to his own shadow, which grew shorter and shorter as he approached a streetlamp, only to grow longer again once he had passed.

On one street a girl stopped him. She smiled, turning her head playfully, and as he continued on he heard a wretched cough that echoed long in the air . . . it was all very hard to understand.

He stopped on the bridge over the Vistula and looked around. A policeman watched him.

"I have a passport," Fliglman thought, and held his hand to his chest.

He stood on the bridge for a long time. From afar he could see two rows of streetlamps whose light formed a fiery L shape. Their reflection shimmered on the surface of the water; clouds of dark and light hues moved across the sky. They seemed to flex and stretch, eventually blending with the water. As traffic passed on the bridge, the whole structure trembled . . . and the darkness crept in ever closer. The clouds descended and everything spun and spun before his eyes, turning without end.

Fliglman felt his whole body shaking and surmised that he must have thrown himself into the water. The shaking seemed to last a long time. He could hear the clattering of wheels on the hard bridge. Something was said to him in Russian, but he did not understand.

He fell asleep at the police station. The whole night he had the sensation that he was lying under water; a bluish stream flowed and flowed before his eyes and he felt light and free. But there was also a throbbing pain at the back of his head, as though he had fallen onto stone.

In the morning, when the policeman pulled him roughly up onto his feet, he had absolutely no memory of how he had gotten there. He looked around with wild, frantic eyes, and when he saw a pair of epaulettes and a sword, and heard a harsh voice, a thought flashed through his mind. He put his hand slowly into his breast pocket and spoke:

"I honorably and humbly beg you, please . . . bury me! I have a passport—look, here it is!"

1905

Higher Education

I

In every group of people there's always that someone who is universally well regarded, with a good reputation, loved by everyone, someone about whom only good things are said and who never seems to have a bad word to say about anyone. In her circle of classmates that person was Lyuba Isakovna Fidler.

Barely a conversation went by without someone referring to her as a "wonderful person!"

Despite her melancholic inclinations—which one noticed in her eager eyes and the sad brevity of her smiles—she was generally in good spirits and ready to take an interest in other people's troubles. She rarely complained. One might think she was the happiest of all her friends, those lost souls who lived a life of dissatisfaction, boredom, and want.

She was a tall, brown-haired girl of about twenty-two with a thin, nimble figure, a pale, somewhat oblong, noble face, and sad, clear eyes. It would be difficult to say that she was extraordinarily beautiful. She was one of those women who are best appreciated by the eye of an artist or a lover, uncovering the harmony and subtle beauty of her features. In the two years since she had moved to Warsaw to study midwifery no one had fallen in love with her, no one had noticed her, and she herself had given up believing that her beauty could please anyone.

A few years ago at *gymnazium* in her hometown in the south of Russia, she had been considered a beauty. She had loved to dress well, and nothing gave her more pleasure than putting on a new, nicely tailored white blouse.

She had been used to receiving favors and infatuated glances and being the best liked. But that was then. Now she was different: appealing for other reasons and in an entirely new way.

She was no better or worse off than any of her friends. Her parents sent her twenty rubles every month—just barely enough for a small attic room on the fourth floor (which she shared with a classmate) and sufficient food to keep hunger at bay. But the twenty rubles didn't always come on time. She knew it wasn't easy for her parents to spare the money, and she felt guilty. Her life consisted of studying, working in the hospital, and reading — mostly clandestine political pamphlets. All that awaited her at the end of the day was a cramped room with slanted walls and a window that opened onto the roof, tea boiled on the stove, and her dear friend Maria Kratova, a Russian from the Moscow region, daughter of a priest. Kratova was a sturdy, well-built creature, good-natured and beautiful, with friendly eyes and timid, sedate movements. She was shy and quiet and very fond of Fidler, but her fondness was more often expressed in a smile or a gesture than in words.

One evening the two girls sat together in their room as the short winter's day was drawing to a close. Darkness was creeping into the narrow room, and the corners were already completely in shadow. They had run out of oil for the lamp and were quietly waiting for a friend who was coming to lend them money for more. Fidler sat by the window, straining her eyes to continue reading her book. Kratova started to stroke Fidler's long hair, braiding and unbraiding it, something that in the full light of day she would not have felt comfortable doing. Fidler continued to read, her eyes battling the ever-expanding darkness.

"Enough reading already; you'll ruin your eyes," said Kratova, her wide smile and gentle face just about visible in the darkness. Fidler stood up, tidied her hair, and picked up a bottle to go find some oil. The friends looked at each other with a smile.

"What do you think, will the shopkeeper let us borrow some oil? I'm going to try."

"That swine won't give you anything," said Kratova. "Don't waste your time. Sit down instead."

The friends sat in the dark, talking openly. Fidler fantasized about her future. Her voice was even softer than usual:

"When I graduate I'm going to apply to work for the *zemstvo*. I'll live in a village somewhere, healing people, being useful in any way I can. I'll spread propaganda. That, my dear, will be a true life, not like here where you could simply die of boredom."

"And you won't get married?" asked Kratova gently.

Fidler thought about it and said: "Yes, why not get married? If I happen to find someone according to my tastes who would be willing to work with me in a village, why not? It's unlikely I'll ever get married though; I'm no beauty, after all. No one is going to fall in love with me, and without love I'll never marry."

"No, you *are* beautiful, I swear it! You're a beauty!"

"You lying scoundrel!" said Fidler, and with that they both burst out laughing.

Such conversations could stretch on for hours, until one of their acquaintances would come and lend them some small change. Now there was light in the room, and for the two friends it seemed as if they had just been living through some sort of dream. They exchanged glances with a smile. Tea was made, soon more acquaintances arrived, everyone spoke, argued, laughed, sang songs, and there was noise and laughter. But Fidler, the most beloved of all, remained strangely subdued and kept herself at a remove. She listened to the conversations but had trouble joining in. She found it curious and irksome to hear such free and easy talk about subjects that she felt were profoundly important, but that she had so few words to describe.

"I'm no hero," she often thought to herself. "I have neither talent nor understanding, but I'll do everything I can to finish my studies and find work in a village."

It had not taken her long to convince herself that she was no hero.

II

Fidler came home from the opera late one night, fired up and invigorated. She found her friend wrapped up in a blanket, sleepy-eyed and shivering with cold. Fidler lit the lamp, loosened the ribbon around her waist, and started excitedly telling Kratova all about the performance she had seen. She had brought her good mood home with her and did not feel like letting go of it just yet. Her ears were still ringing with the sound of the music, her head was still spinning from the colorful images, whereas in her room it was just so dreary and dark.

"I met a young man at the opera this evening," she told her drowsy friend, "a strange bourgeois with a gold watch, a bit of a dandy. He was quite gallant, I assure you! He offered me his seat and paid me so many compliments; oh, how pathetic it was! Batistini sang so divinely, and there I was, sitting like a lady, with my cavalier standing behind in a corner."

All she wanted to do was talk, but Kratova was tired. Fidler fell silent and retreated into her thoughts. Through some wondrous association she was reminded of the old days when she was a schoolgirl. The merry flickering and crackling of the torches as the orchestra played; how she glided so happily, how loudly she laughed, and how people whispered compliments in her ear . . . her mind overflowed with excitement.

Soon the two friends were in the bed that they shared.

"You know what, Maria?" Fidler said, waking her friend up. "He's actually quite well educated, a doctor."

She had just remembered that he had introduced himself as Dr. Vaynshteyn.

"Who are you talking about?" asked Kratova, half asleep.

"My cavalier, of course, the one who let me have his seat. Are you asleep?"

"Yes, my love, let me sleep."

A carriage drove by on the street, causing the windowpanes to tremble. The bell rang at the gate below.

"Shhh!" There were footsteps. Was someone coming to search the house and have them arrested?

"What sort of thoughts are creeping into my head today!" she chided herself.

It was normal that the opera excited her. It was her usual release from mundane routine. But today there was also a new feeling: the young man, the compliments, the fact that someone liked her . . .

And still, the following day she did not feel as though she had returned to the humdrum. It was not like before.

But what use are the dreams that pass through the minds of the lonely, disappearing just as quickly as they arrive? Fidler would have already forgotten about the whole story had she not—as she was walking through the streets one day at her usual fast pace—happened to see that very same "dandy and cavalier," Dr. Vaynshteyn. He was a man in his early thirties, with an intelligent, yet somewhat dull, face, and a thick, blond mustache. On either side of his face were two deep creases near his mouth, with other smaller wrinkles around his large, clear eyes.

He was strolling deliberately down the street. They both stopped reluctantly, smiling at each other. He was pleased to run into her, and when he asked where she was going and learned that she was on her way home, he offered to accompany her.

"But don't hurry; I don't like to rush," he said.

Like all young people, Fidler had a lot of questions, and Dr. Vayshteyn was glad to answer them. She discovered that he was the son of very rich parents who lived out in the country in a village in the Kovno region. Dr. Vaynshteyn told her he'd lived abroad for many years, working as a medical doctor, but that he no longer practiced medicine: for the time being he was "just living" here in Warsaw. He pronounced these words with a half smile, in which there lay some self-deprecating irony. Fidler looked at him in puzzlement and asked: "What do you do here then?"

"It's hard to say. Nothing."

"Nothing?"

"Nothing," he answered with the same smile. "Does that surprise you? I'm rich; I mean to say: I have rich parents. Necessity does not drive to me work, nor does any inner desire, for that matter. I'm a professional bourgeois," he joked.

"But isn't that a little tiresome?"

"A little tiresome, yes."

When they reached her door, he thought for a moment and said: "I would like to meet you more often, if I may."

"What for?" she asked, a little curious, a little flirtatious, looking straight into his face with her wide, sad eyes.

"Only to keep boredom at bay. No, really," he added in a serious tone, "I'm a stranger here in Warsaw, I have practically no intelligent friends, and it would be my pleasure to meet up with you."

Despite his "untalented nature" (he described himself as someone who was of no use to others and lived without any enjoyment on his part), Vaynshteyn had one great virtue, which sometimes made him very likeable: when he wanted to, he could be serious, childishly earnest, and openhearted. In those moments his tone lost its characteristic irony, and his facial expressions also became different. He had uttered those last words to Fidler in this serious tone, and in that moment Fidler liked him.

"It's possible," she replied. "If you want, come up to my place, but I'll be honest with you, I'm not sure you'll like my room. You being a bourgeois and all."

"Oh, don't talk nonsense."

But in her room their conversation floundered. He told her about his student days abroad and made jokes about how cramped and dark the room was—he found that crooked walls were more interesting, because they were richer in lines and corners. But his jokes fell flat, and as soon as Kratovka came home he said his goodbyes and left.

"You know," Fidler told Kratovka, "that's the same doctor I met at the opera. A very interesting, cultivated man."

"A social revolutionary?"

"No. He doesn't seem to do anything in particular, but he's still interesting. He's bored and is looking for companionship with intelligent people."

Kratova seemed skeptical.

"What?" asked Fidler. "What don't you understand?"

"Let's hope he's not a spy, at least."

"Oh shut up! You don't even know him."

And with that Fidler brought the conversation to a close.

A few days later she received a ticket along with a letter from Dr. Vaynshteyn inviting her to join him to see an opera by Wagner.

"You're very kind," she said somewhat ironically. "I wanted to see Wagner so badly. It's terrible how much I love him! And to tell the truth I didn't have any money. You came to my rescue; thank you!"

Out of the whole monologue, the final "thank you" came out so freely and naturally that they both felt at ease.

What a joyous evening it was! Normally when she went to the opera her seat was on the top balcony, where she was forced to stand most of the time, keeping her balance so as not to fall. It was in such a pose that she had first caught the attention of Dr. Vatnshtayn. She had been standing on her seat, holding on to a pole for balance, and her bent, slender figure had possessed a particular charm.

Now she sat by the stage, free, undisturbed. And Vaynshteyn seemed more affable than before. He sat calmly, a somewhat austere expression on his face, and there she noticed for the first time a deep, old sadness, a sadness so entwined with him it seemed as though he could not have been created without it.

Later they went to a café. As always after the opera, Fidler was in an energetic, happy mood. She felt that there was still so much brightness, so much splendor in the world.

"How pleasant it is to have money!" she thought. Her eyes sparkled, her light, agile body looked even fresher, more graceful. She noticed how glances came at her from all directions. Dr. Vaynshteyn, on the other hand, sat with a weary expression, seemingly exhausted.

"You have no idea what sort of milieu I grew up in, and still live in," he suddenly began, as if seeking to justify his sadness to her.

"Our Jewish bourgeoisie—that's the worst you could possibly imagine: crude, depraved, godless, tasteless, without style, without traditions, without a future. Only one thing matters to them, only one pursuit interests them, and that's money. Imagine, I spent eight years abroad, living by my own means. I observed life around me, I studied, read, and developed myself; in short, I strived to become what we call 'cultivated.' Now it turns out that this is not a virtue but a vice! Naturally, the fact that I have a medical degree pleases my family—not that it has any practical use, not for me and not for others—but they can't stand my philosophy and look on me as a low-life, an idler.

"They can only think of one way to save me: marriage. It's laughable, but it causes me such pain. All my aunts feel duty-bound to make me happy and find me a potential bride. They practically never leave me alone.

"It's become so intolerable that I've stopped visiting them altogether, which caused a scandal. My father is angry, my mother sends me tear-stained letters, my aunts pester me constantly . . . I have no other choice, it seems, than to go abroad again."

He finished his long monologue and gazed at her searchingly.

Clearly he himself didn't understand why he was telling her all this.

"There are so few happy people in this world," he concluded, "and I'm jealous of those who have some sort of goal, who can forget about themselves. They feel good; they have no worries and only think about others, and that's it."

Fidler sighed, glad that he had finished.

Dr. Vaynshteyn changed the subject, managing to leave the uncomfortable conversation behind, and they stayed in the café a while longer, talking about opera, Warsaw, and other uncomplicated things. It was already very late by the time he brought her home, and as he was saying goodbye he held her hand tightly.

"Are you going abroad soon?" she asked.

"Not yet. Not so soon," he answered, and the sad weariness of his face was hidden by an affable smile.

III

Fidler wasn't in love with Vaynshteyn, she was sure of that much. Nevertheless she enjoyed meeting up with him and listening to him speak. Lately she had even taken to visiting him in his apartment, although she had long resisted it.

"What do I actually have in common with him?" she thought. "Why go home with him anyway? There's no need for it." But Vaynshteyn had asked her to come over several times, and she didn't want to offend him (in general whenever she spoke to him she was afraid of offending him with a misplaced word).

"Well, I never imagined an emancipated woman should have to worry about such nonsense!" he said with his usual kindly but cold smile. "What? You're afraid to visit me in my home?"

She had nothing to answer to that.

One afternoon, Vaynshteyn heard two knocks at his door. He rose to answer it, and in walked Fidler. Vaynshteyn shook her hand, and his face radiated so much satisfaction that Fidler couldn't help but notice. She smiled.

"I knew it was you from the way you knocked: such quiet, determined knocks . . ." he said with a laugh.

"And I, Mr. Vaynshteyn, have only come for a minute. I want to borrow something to read," she said.

"Well, come in then, come in . . . sit down in the meantime."

She truly intended to stay for just a minute; she didn't know what to talk about or how to behave with him in general. She had imagined that it would be awkward, like that time when he had sat in her room, but she was wrong. On the contrary, she felt quite at ease in his large, bright, tastefully furnished apartment. Vaynshteyn had an office and a bedroom. He also appeared fresher and younger when he was at home. He was wearing his usual work clothes, and his hair was a little messy—just the right amount of messiness for a busy person. Books in several languages lay on the table, some of them already opened, some of them brand new, along with journals and loose illustrations. He showed them to her, explaining each item in turn, and she responded by saying, "Very interesting, very interesting," quite glad that she had not been wrong about him, that he truly was a cultivated man.

"Oh! You have one of those too?" she said, pointing to a rocking chair. She went over and sat down on it.

"It's lovely!" she said, rocking herself slowly on the chair. She liked it, and she was as happy as a child. He stood next to her and was charmed by the lovely young thing for whom there was still so much joy in the world, so many things to be happy about.

But then she bolted up, as if suddenly remembering something, and frowned. She felt as though she had already let things go too far.

"What exactly am I doing here with him anyway?" she asked herself, and found no answer.

"Well, I should go. Goodbye," she said.

He didn't try to stop her. There was something in her expression and in her tone that told him it would be unwise.

"Goodbye, then," he said. "You see? I'm not trying to stop you. But you must promise to come again. You'll come again, won't you?"

"We'll see," she answered coldly.

"No. Promise me you'll come."

Once again Fidler was afraid that she might offend him, and so she promised.

She began to visit regularly, and, while they enjoyed many good, carefree moments, there were also tedious, difficult moments, where the conversation did not run so smoothly and they felt the full distance, in education, in age, and in status, that stood between them.

One visit in particular stood out: she was sitting on the rocking chair, rocking, while he told her a story that caused him some embarrassed amusement:

"I have a sister-in-law here in Warsaw—she is the educated one in our family. She took courses, understands several languages, and used to be interested in many things. What has become of her now? That's another question. At any rate she has claims of being educated and, what's more, she's an attractive woman. In short: we pinned all of our hopes on her. She intends to make somebody out of me, and that means finding me a wife with a large dowry."

"They're trying to arrange your marriage?" Fidler laughed. It was warm and comfortable in the room, the winter sun peeking in through the window, and she was in a good mood.

"Now listen, and don't laugh. A few days ago she told me—with quite a serious expression—that I should come over to her place for tea the following evening. 'Wear an overcoat,' she whispered into my ear, 'there will be guests.'

"Of course I went—in this very jacket! You can just imagine the scene: An older lady was sitting there at the table, and she was with a girl, clearly her daughter, my future fiancée that is, and my sister-in-law Sonia. The latter, seeing me dressed like this, was somewhat confused. But she is a capable woman, skillful; she tried to turn the story around. 'We weren't expecting you today,' she said to me. She turned to the girl and introduced me in French. The poor thing went red up to the ears, and I, if you can picture it, tried to start up a conversation—in Yiddish! You should have seen the nasty look my sister gave me. I fear she won't feel the need to play matchmaker with me from now on."

"Oh stop, you're so mean!" Fidler said, laughing loudly, and she didn't recognize her own voice.

That day she was especially beautiful: fresh, childishly playful. The special charm of her figure, which Vaynshteyn had found so pleasing that first time at the opera, called out to be embraced, and to be caressed . . .

"Allow me, I'd like to rock you," he said and started to rock the chair.

But it was a step too far. She fixed him with a stern expression, all trace of childlike playfulness gone from her eyes. Again he noticed a warning in her look. She soon got up, coldly said goodbye, and left.

There was a jumble of feelings and thoughts in her head. Most of all she could not answer the question: for what rhyme or reason had she gone to his place? He is not like her and is probably just laughing at her. And when she thought like that, remembering his dull face and cold smile—the smile of a person who had already tasted all the love and happiness that the world had to offer—she felt something like hatred awakening in her heart, toward him and his cold smile.

"He's not even handsome either," she said to herself, as if seeking to take revenge on a person who can smile coldly at the sort of feelings that fell upon her like a storm, robbing her of her breath.

But the cramped room at home was becoming tediously claustrophobic, and her heartfelt friendship with Kratova was not as strong as it had once been. There was now a third presence in the room with them: Fidler's uneasy conscience.

"Would you be able to marry someone you didn't love?" she asked her friend once.

"Don't be silly! Who could do a thing like that?"

"I wouldn't be able to either," Fidler said quietly, as if talking to her own heart. A little later she asked, "What do you think: could you love a man who has already loved many, many times before, who has already had a lot of women?"

"Pfui! That's nasty!" Kratova answered.

"I don't like men like that either," Fidler said, sinking deep in thought, remembering every little detail on Vaynshteyn's face.

Dr. Vaynshteyn—on the very day that she had been with him, when he had told her the story of the matchmaking—wrote a long letter to a friend of his in Berlin. He felt very close to that friend, a sickly, poor Jewish painter. He wrote in detail about his situation, and mentioned Fidler many times:

> To ease my boredom, I have made the acquaintance of a student here, a Jewish girl, a revolutionary, a lovely creature, gracious, clever, and entirely truthful. More than anything, though, she's young, so very young! Everything sounds good when she says it, even when she comes out with clichéd platitudes. She is finishing up her course in midwifery and wants to move to a village and heal Russian peasants; she intends to turn them into revolutionaries. When I made fun of her she lost her temper, spouting a lot of nonsense, and yet it's so lovely to listen to, you can only imagine.

Don't get me wrong: I am not in love with her. But this much is true: if I have to marry someone, I would not take anyone from the Russian-Jewish bourgeois circles. I look at her sometimes and think: if I do have a child, it could only be with someone like her.

And yet—if you believe me—there are times when I look at her and am shocked. I feel like an animal, a predator. I don't know how to put this, but I am already thirty-four years old. My heart is cold, and there she is—a young, fresh girl, with all of her youthful convictions, with all of her hopes. All of which could belong to me, because . . . because I am rich. So base, stupid, inhuman, is it not?

Well, if she were at least in love with me, that would be different, but she is not. I feel it in her words, the way she looks at me. And yet—perhaps I am mistaken?

What can a broken, Jewish bourgeois like me have to offer, apart from doubts?

Anyway . . . same old stories. Fidler—that's her name—is a lovely, beautiful creature. I miss her right now . . .

IV

"Don't try to pull the wool over my eyes, Alexander. I know what's going on. I know what it means when you say you don't want to get married. What is there to hide? Tell me, please, when will I have the honor of meeting her? No really, will you introduce me to her?"

So spoke Madame Sonia, Dr. Alexander Vaynshteyn's sister-in-law, an attractive, still youthful woman, a brunette with light, shining eyes and a typically Jewish face. Even though they were alone, she was dressed with taste and a hint of coquettishness. Her blouse was quite low cut, she wore a thin red band on her neck, diamonds sparked from her ears, and several rings shone upon her fingers. She smiled often, opening her lower lip to reveal healthy, white teeth.

"Where did Sonia get such an idea? Who said that?" Dr. Vaynshteyn protested.

"Please Alexander, don't mock me. I'm not a stranger after all. I want to know my future sister-in-law. What is it? You're ashamed? Or afraid of being disturbed? No, you really have to introduce us. You must, you simply must!"

She slapped the table twice with her small hand and smiled, showing her teeth again.

Dr. Vaynshteyn didn't answer. He looked at her small, amply adorned hand and asked, "Oh! Sonia has a new ring? Let me see."

She spoke informally to him, but he rarely reciprocated, often addressing her in the third person. She stretched out her round, nicely filled, feminine fingers toward him, revealing the glittering stone in their midst.

"You act just like a stranger toward us. Did you not hear that Yefim won the Przepiórka case? Seven thousand eight hundred rubles, plus court costs. He had promised to buy me this if he won. But you have no interest in what goes on in this house—a fine brother you are!"

"But you see, I *am* interested," he joked, slipping the ring back onto her finger. "Just now I noticed that Sonia had a new ring. How many rings do you own now? Let's count; looks like soon you'll have more rings than fingers."

"Stop it, Alexander. I know you're a born socialist, and your new *friend* is also a socialist. I know everything, everything!"

"Then why ask if one knows everything already?" remarked Vaynshteyn angrily.

She suddenly laughed playfully.

"Out comes the anger!" she said. "Do you think you can keep secrets? Everyone knows, and people are constantly asking me about it wherever I go."

Dr. Vaynshteyn wondered to himself. He did not have much of a social life in Warsaw, so he didn't understand where the rumors could have come from.

"Who are they, this *everyone*?" he said loudly and severely. "And who told you such a story? Who is so worried about me? I thought I didn't know anyone here, apart from you and my brother."

"Who cares who *you* know. They know *you*," Sonia answered, also in a serious tone, and she named several houses where they had spoken about him, where they had told her with complete certainty that Dr. Vaynshteyn had a fiancée. He couldn't get his head around it; how did she know with such accuracy what Fidler looked like, that she was a student, a revolutionary? She even knew which days they had been to the philharmonic together, when they had been to the opera, how and where he had walked with her.

"Well, well!" he shook his head. "I had no idea I was so popular. You have to admit, they really know how to spy on you here; I would never have imagined."

He was silent for a moment. Sonia looked at him with a mischievous smile, as if to say, "Now that you've admitted it, you may as well tell me the whole story."

"No, sister-in-law," Dr. Vaynshteyn insisted, "don't believe these rumors. I don't have a fiancée. As for that person, she really is a very nice girl, a good friend of mine, and I like talking with her."

"You're lying, Alexander!" she wagged her finger at him. "Come now; you're lying!"

"I swear, it's nothing serious at all," he protested, but he had shocked her by swearing.

"Nothing serious?" he asked himself. He thought deeply, furrowing his brow.

A thought occurred to him; he knew that Fidler had terrible financial worries, but he wasn't brazen enough to offer her money. No matter how he did it, it would offend her. But she had once mentioned that she was looking for private students, and now he saw an opportunity to let Sonia get what she wanted.

"By the way," he said, "if Sonia is interested, there is one way that she could get to know her. The girl is looking for students; perhaps you know someone in need of a tutor?"

"There, you see? That's what I'm talking about," Sonia was delighted. "I wanted to find a Russian teacher for my Boris . . ."

"Before this moment you wanted no such thing," thought Dr. Vaynshteyn, but he said nothing.

Yefim, Dr. Vaynshteyn's brother, entered the room. He was a tall, well-built man of about forty, with a receding hairline and small eyes behind a pair of golden glasses. He was clean-shaven, except for the very end of his chin, where he cultivated a patch of short hairs. He enjoyed stroking these hairs with his fingers whenever his mind was under strain. He entered as usual, silently and unnoticed, without greeting anyone. He sat down at the table and started reading the newspaper. Reading the news was a form of relaxation for him, a retreat from his business, from buying, selling, exchanging, from meetings and speculation, from all those things that never stopped spinning around inside his head.

"Do you want to eat?" Sonia asked.

"Not yet," he answered quietly.

He put aside the newspaper, apparently only just then noticing his brother.

"If you're traveling abroad again, let me know," he said, turning to Alexander. "I can get you a cheap passport; I have connections."

"He's not going away so quickly," Sonia replied, looking at her brother-in-law with a smile.

Yefim didn't answer and went back to his newspaper, but Sonia snatched the paper from his hands and said, "He comes home for a minute and can't take the time to say a word." Yefim could already tell from her tone that there was something she wanted, and he prepared himself to hear all about it. He raised his head, stuck his fingers into the spiky hairs on his chin, and asked with humor in his voice, "What do you want, my dear?"

"I want you to talk to me," she said in a chirpy tone, "and I want to get a Russian teacher for Boris."

"Well, where is he then, asleep already?"

Sonia went into the other room, and a minute later she was back, leading by the hand a beautiful, blond seven-year-old. With full, round cheeks and a fresh haircut, the boy was half ready for bed. He tore himself away from his mother's hand and was delighted that he had been freed from having to go to sleep. He went up to his father with bold steps and kissed his hand.

"*Dobry wieczór,*" he said in Polish—ever since the children had come along the Vaynshteyns had added Polish, along with Russian, to their linguistic repertoire. His father picked him up, lifted him onto his lap, and stroked his head.

"Tell us something Boris, how are things?"

"Good," the little one said in a practical tone of voice, and shook his head. "The teacher gave me a four today."

"We're going to find you a new teacher for Russian; would you like that?" Sonia said.

"I would, but please tell her that she shouldn't give me too much homework," Boris said with the same practical tone. "I don't have the time." Everyone laughed except Boris, who only understood that he had said something clever but didn't know why it was so amusing. They got ready for dinner. The governess appeared at the door: an old German woman with a pale, withered face who called out: "Boris, bed!"

But Boris didn't want to leave the company. Alexander stood up for him: "Leave him be, he's a good lad. He'll grow up to be a respectable man, a merchant or a lawyer like his father—not a philosopher at any rate."

Sonia took him to her side and they started to eat. Boris was soon lying with his head on her chest. His eyes had closed; he could no longer resist sleep and dozed off. His mother held him, looking into his sleeping face with a contented, maternal expression. She seemed nicer now, more sympathetic, more authentic and beautiful. Alexander recognized the Sonia from the old days, whom he'd met just after the wedding when he went traveling with her husband. She made an agreeable impression on him in that moment. To have a child who falls asleep like that on its mother's breast wouldn't be so bad, he thought, and he remembered what he had written in the letter to his friend that time: if he were to have a child, it could only be with her.

"So should the young lady come?"

"Absolutely, absolutely," she answered with a smile. Half an hour later he was out on the street. It was a fine frosty winter's night around nine o'clock. He came out of the gate, stopped, and looked around.

"Where am I going?"

He was in the habit of going to bed late and didn't feel like returning home to his lonely apartment to read. It was already too late to go to the theater. He let himself be led by the crowds who were still out walking. How great it would be if he just happened to bump into her in the street. But he didn't see her. He wandered for a couple of hours, sat in a café for a while, and finally went home to bed, unsatisfied.

"What was the point of arranging those lessons with my sister-in-law?" he thought. "She doesn't even need lessons and is only doing it out of curiosity. Fidler would no doubt be deeply offended if she knew that I was luring her in order to show her off.

"It's always like that," he continued. "I can never do things the right way, always pettiness, always doing things by halves, no power, no courage—low, ugly!"

Such and similar thoughts were whispered to him by his loneliness. As usual, he laid all the blame on his Jewish origins. "A lowly race," he cursed.

First thing in the morning he sent Fidler a note, calling her "Dear Lyuba" for the first time, instead of the more formal "*Sehr geehrte* Fidler."

> Please go to Marszałkowska number . . . there's a private student there for you. You see, I haven't forgotten about you. You must come. I miss you.
>
> Yours,
> Dr. A. Vaynshteyn

And a few days later, Fidler went to the first of what would become regular one o'clock visits to the Vaynshteyns. On her way out of the room where she taught little Boris, she met Dr. Vaynshteyn, who had been waiting for her.

V

Fidler spent the whole winter living between two worlds. On one side there were her friends, her classmates, her studies, the hospital, and the cramped room; on the other side there was Dr. Vaynshteyn, his sister-in-law, little Boris, the theater, and the cafés. On one side, her clear purpose: finishing her studies and settling in a village; on the other side, a murky expectation. Between those two worlds there could be no harmony, and she found no way out. She suffered uneasily and in silence.

It's better not to think anything at all, she decided, but still the thoughts came into her head unbidden.

She felt that by crossing a few streets and entering Dr. Vaynshteyn's world she became another person. She spoke differently there, laughed differently, she even thought differently; completely different ideas came into her head and completely different words came out of her mouth. But in her own room, with her friends at the hospital, she had also changed.

She wasn't the only one to notice it: there was gossip about her. If one of her old friends referred to Fidler now, like they used to, as a "wonderful person," they would more than likely be greeted by skepticism. True, she was the same agreeable, kind Fidler as before. The same intelligent, longing expression, the same warm smile on her lips, the same willingness to take an interest in other people's worries. And yet she was different: a stranger to her friends. Those who are held up as an exemplar without vices lose everything as soon as a single stain is discovered. That's how it was with Fidler; everyone suddenly felt that they had misjudged her all along.

The ringleader of her little group, an older, not particularly good-looking student by the name of Esfir, came into Fidler's room one night to deliver a packet of freshly printed pamphlets and proclamations. Instead of giving the package straight to Fidler, as she had done in the past, she now gave it to Kratova and told her to distribute as many of them as she could around the hospital and to hide the rest. She then turned to Fidler and asked: "How goes it with your patron?"

Fidler went red with insult and felt the tears welling up in her eyes.

"What sort of patron is he to me?" she answered, before realizing that Esfir had not even mentioned him by name. "Am I forbidden from having friends? I don't understand."

"Who said, my dear, that it's forbidden? As far as I'm concerned you should go ahead and marry him; why not? He'd make a good match for you." And without waiting for a response from Fidler she said goodbye and walked toward the door.

"Anyway, I have no time for chitchat," she said as she left. Fidler felt the sharp stab of offense in her heart.

She saw Dr. Vaynshteyn almost every day. Either he was there waiting after her lessons at his sister-in-law's place, or she came by his place. Sometimes the time would pass pleasantly. As she sat in his rocking chair he told her stories that made her laugh and forget about everything. She felt that whatever she did was pleasing, that her words were well placed and that her laughter, far from disturbing anyone, spread joy. Sometimes he stood behind her, pushing the rocking chair slowly and gently, as one would rock a child. There wasn't much standing in the way of him leaning over and kissing her. She was expecting it, and the idea frightened her; she was not sure what she would do it he did.

"No, he won't allow himself to behave like that with me," she decided, and yet she peered into his face and tried to find more sympathy in it, more beauty, something more in tune with her desires.

"What's this plan of yours to settle in a village anyway?" he asked. "You'll wither away there and come to nothing, surrounded by peasants who are completely alien to you. It's a waste of your youth, your beauty lost out in the backwaters around Arkhangelsk. At the very least you should be with other workers in a city with some culture. That I could understand; that at least is modern. But what makes you, a Jewish girl, want to live with Russian peasants? No, you won't do that."

She only smiled and said, "You're so sure that I won't do it! Let's not talk about it then. I don't like it when you talk like that." Her expression was serious as she said it.

But she felt in his words, his gaze, and his whole behavior toward her that he now loved her, and sooner or later she would inevitably become his wife.

Become his wife! The thought frightened her; there was so much about him that was unusual, and she wasn't sure why it terrified her so: because it made her sad, or because it made her happy?

She noticed that during her lessons at the Vaynshteyns' they treated her differently, not like a normal teacher. Sonia would come into the room where she taught little Boris and speak about the exercises, chatting and wasting time for no reason. Fidler felt as if she were always under Sonia's watchful gaze, that there was so much curiosity and something of a hidden smile in those black eyes. Once, just as she was leaving at the end of the lesson, Sonia suddenly appeared in the doorway and said, half serious, half in jest: "Wait a minute; Alexander will be here soon."

Fidler blushed and curtly replied that she had no time. She hurried to leave.

Everyone liked her in the house. Fidler felt it and wasn't surprised. She was used to making a good impression; it was a part of her, like art to an artist or good looks to a famous actress. Even little Boris liked her and was happy when she came; consequently, though, he hated his German governess all the more.

"And why do I like Panna Lyuba? Because Panna Lyuba is kind and the Fräulein is bad." That was his assessment when his mother scolded him for some conflict between him and his governess.

Sonia told all this to Fidler and asked, "Tell me please, why do children like you so terribly much?"

Sonia looked deep into Fidler's somewhat long face and couldn't for the life of her figure out what was so beautiful about it.

"Pleasant, nothing more," she thought. In her heart she looked on Fidler with contempt, underestimating her, and yet she treated her well and spoke to her as to an equal. She enjoyed the role she was playing in Alexander's affairs. She couldn't allow him to get married without her playing a part. She also wanted to get her husband involved:

"What do you say about our Alexander?" she asked her husband. "He seems to have fallen in love with our teacher . . ."

He only shrugged his shoulders and answered coldly: "Well, he should marry her then."

"Marry her? Haha! What an idea; have you gone mad? She is a poor girl, a midwife."

"Do you want to hear me, Sonia, or not? Listen to me and don't get involved. You won't be able to change things either way. He's crazy after all, and if you say no, he'll say yes."

But Sonia could not rest. She wrote to her in-laws about it, dropping hints about her brother-in-law's behavior, and she kept herself busy by spying on all parties.

On one occasion she confronted Fidler about Alexander.

"How do you like Alexander?" she asked. "Do you think he's really a good person?"

Fidler blushed and answered with an undecided expression.

Sonia continued, "He's a very good person. But do you know, he's quite strange. Tell me, why did he study medicine if he didn't want to become a doctor? What good did it do him? You know he stands to inherit thirty thousand rubles?" She paused to see what impression those last words would make. Her black, cunning eyes looked at Fidler, and Fidler noticed, for the first time, a bitterness in those cold eyes.

"Medicine is quite an interesting science; why not study it if you have the opportunity?" she remarked curtly and stood up, getting ready to leave.

"Wait, Alexander will be here any minute."

And again Fidler noticed the coldness and contempt in her eyes and was silent.

"Oh, how cruel she is, how bourgeois she is," she thought as she left. She felt growing hatred for this dark woman with her long, chiseled nose, with her black, curved eyebrows and cold gaze. It was the blind hatred that seizes a woman so quickly when someone stands in her way, a silent hatred, unspoken and burning. And yet she had to come to this woman's house every day, talk to her, smile, put on a good face. It wore her down more with each passing day. When she remembered her plan to go to the village, her heart gave a tremble and her head spun: "Terrible, terrible!" And again she sat on the rocking chair at Dr. Vaynshteyn's place as he spoke kind words to her in his soft voice and looked at her with enamored eyes, and she was once again happy, laughing and laughing. He took her hand in his. She wanted to protest but said nothing. He kissed her hair, touching her forehead softly with his lips. She wanted to scream and yet she didn't scream.

Only when she got home to her room and started reading the pamphlets and talking to Kratova was her heart once again heavy, her thoughts once again in turmoil.

It was terrible to contemplate the good fortune that awaited her: the prospect of comfort and wealth. Terrible too was the thought that she would marry a man whom she, perhaps, did not love. The doubt oppressed her that the whole thing was just a game to him, and he would abandon her. On the other hand, it was equally terrible to envision a life full of need, boredom, and scarcity; but the shame she felt in front of her friends and her own conscience, that was the most terrible thing of all.

On the door of her room hung a new, expensive silk blouse. The blouse had a story behind it. A world famous artist had come to perform at the theater. Sonia had booked a loge seat for herself, her husband, and Dr. Vaynshteyn. Fidler was to be the fourth member of their party. When Dr. Vaynshteyn invited her to come with them to the theater, to sit with them in the loge, she thought he was joking. When he brought it up again, she only laughed.

"Don't talk nonsense! That's all I need—in the loge, dressed like this!"

He didn't respond, but as they continued down the street and passed by an expensive women's-wear shop, he stopped and practically forced her to buy something.

"You've earned it after all your teaching. I'll pay this time."

That's how the blouse came to be bought. Later, in the theater, she had felt self-conscious under Sonia's gaze and that of her husband, who had stared at her through his glasses without saying a word. Fidler could not look at that blouse dispassionately. It seemed to stand for everything that had changed in her.

"Do you know what I'm going to do?" she said to Kratova. "Tomorrow, I'm going to take the blouse to the pawn shop. I'll get enough for it to pay for lunch."

"No, you shouldn't. It suits you so well. You look really good in it."

"You're making fun of me; you don't like me anymore, do you? Say something . . ." said Fidler, and with those last words, her voice trembled.

But Kratova didn't answer. She just wiped her thick hand over Fidler's forehead with a lazy movement and said, "You're a fool, you know that?" And on her face lay a broad, calm, Russian smile.

VI

Winter was coming to an end, and the pre-spring days arrived, bringing with them their new winds, soft and fresh, which invigorate the air, lending a sweet uneasiness to everything. Nature became unsettled—unsettled and regretful.

Having long since shaken off the last of the snow, the trees in the city gardens swayed calmly with their bare branches, waiting and drinking in the good green moss which would come at night to kiss and fertilize them. The clouds filed past quickly as if in a hurry to fix something, to prepare something. The sky looked out from behind them and the sun was warm—a newborn, blue sky, a newborn, dear sun.

And the nights were full of longing and nervous hope. There was a light frost. The pavements were slippery, the thin ice crackled pleasantly underfoot, and the mild wind awakened every nerve, stirring up the blood in one's veins.

Somewhere, far off in the deep forest, the bear awoke in its den, filling the woods with wild bellows. In the city human hearts trembled, and interrupted dreams started to spin again. It was an unsettled, dangerous time for young hearts.

Fidler returned home well after midnight. She undressed and got into bed, but she could not sleep. Kratova was already asleep and didn't even notice Fidler coming in and lying down next to her in bed. There was a kindly, satisfied smile on her face, her high, full breast moving slowly, so calm and peaceful. Not a muscle budged on her face; clearly she wasn't even dreaming. Her young, blossoming body seemed to be waiting without worry, trepidation, or longing for her predestined one, who must and would come.

Fidler re-lit the lamp. She felt constrained in the bed and the stuffy room. She had a strong urge to laugh aloud or weep, to scream for fear, or pour out her heart and confide in someone.

"My God, my God!" she sighed.

Why were all her nerves on edge? What was it that pressed on her heart? What sort of poison had stirred up her blood? What should she do? What was she going to do? Why had her life become so confusing?

And she fantasized about a young man with black hair, with glowing eyes and powerful hands, who would come and embrace her—firmly embrace her—so that her every limb should feel his youthful strength. And he, her noble savior, would carry her far, far away in his arms, to the village where she would reawaken, where life would be so happy and clean and beautiful.

But just then she heard the front doorbell ringing down below, and Fidler was afraid. She felt ashamed of her fear. She remembered that fear had once been alien to her, but lately she had begun feeling more and more afraid.

She listened anxiously to what was happening below; someone was coming up the stairs, several people. They had already reached the second floor and still did not stop.

"Is it really happening?" she thought in fright.

She woke up her friend.

"Maria, I think they're coming for us . . ."

But Kratova did not wake up until the footsteps were very close and there was a knock on the door.

"Who's there?" Fidler asked.

"A telegram," came the reply.

Kratova woke up suddenly, her eyes wide open, and she looked frantically around, trying to figure out what was happening. After hearing the word "telegram" everything was immediately clear. She jumped out of bed and hastily dressed.

"We'll break down the door and shoot, open this minute!"

"Can we?" Kratova asked Fidler, who was putting on her shoe. But the banging on the door became so loud that they were left with no other option but to open up. In came a gendarme officer, tall and pale, with a very long mustache, followed by several policemen and the caretaker from their building. The room became crowded.

The search had begun.

"So I'm being arrested," thought Fidler. "Well fine, at least it's an end, at least something will change."

And yet her heart beat loudly. Her mouth was horribly dry all of a sudden, and even when simply asked to give her name, she answered with a trembling voice. Kratova on the other hand answered calmly, and only her wide-open eyes hinted at her agitation.

The officer did not have to search for long. He soon found some pamphlets in a drawer. He looked them over, read the titles, and smiled with satisfaction.

"We have you now," he said, pulling at his mustache and looking at the two girls with a smile. "Who do they belong to?" he asked sternly.

"They are mine," Fidler wanted to say, but she said nothing. She imagined that she had moved her lips, that she had uttered the words, but no sound came out of her mouth. Instead she heard loud and clear as Kratova said, "They're mine."

And the officer answered: "Good."

"She wants to take the blame herself and let me free," Fidler thought. "No, no! It can't happen like this, by no means."

She stood and stared, eager to act.

"Is that yours, Kratova?" the officer asked. "And you? What are you hiding, Fidler? Better show us right away; it will save us from searching. It would be a shame to waste time."

Fidler answered defiantly: "Search if you want."

The police started raking through every corner. The officer ordered them to look in the stove, in the bed, under the bed, to knock on the walls, but they found nothing more. Kratova stood still the whole time next to the table. Aware that she was being arrested, it seemed as if she could no longer move. Fidler sat on the bed, her head spinning.

"No, no, it can't happen like this!" she thought. "I have to say that they're mine." And she prepared to do so, but she did not know how. Then a different thought came into her head: it wouldn't help Kratova anyway. Instead of one victim, there would be two. Perhaps they were going to arrest both of them anyway. She would find out soon enough.

Suddenly Kratova turned to face her. Their eyes met, and at that moment Fidler felt a burning pain in her heart. "What shame, what shame, I'm a vile hypocrite, a traitor!" she cursed herself.

The official documentation finished, the officer read it over and got everyone to sign it. Fidler knew for certain now that Kratova was being arrested, and she was being left free, so she made one last effort: "Take me too!" she said to the officer.

But he just calmly stroked his mustache again and answered, "The time will come when we will take you too. For now enjoy your freedom. And you—madame," he turned to Kratova, "get dressed if you would; we're going."

Kratova put on her jacket and went to say goodbye to Fidler. Her eyes shone with joy; clearly she had already made peace with the idea that she was being arrested, and she was happy and proud to have handled herself so well.

"Farewell," she said. "Write home if they ask about me, but tell them that I will soon be free. Remember." And they kissed goodbye.

"Stay safe, my dear," said Fidler, wanting to justify herself but incapable of speaking. She suddenly broke down into tears.

"Forgive me, forgive me," she stammered. "I'm a hypocrite, a vile hypocrite . . ."

They led Kratova away. As she was leaving she turned around and looked at Fidler; in her eyes was the same gleam, and for a moment a look of pride flashed across her face. Fidler still wanted to go to her, but just then Kratova stepped over the threshold, followed by the officer and the police.

Fidler was left alone in her room, alone with her heavy conscience, alone with her tears. Her new blouse still beckoned from the wall.

The few hours until dawn stretched on like an eternity. She paced up and down, gripping her temples until she fell exhausted onto her bed, then covered her face with a pillow and wept. The lamp, which she had already refilled with the last of the oil, was on the verge of going out, and the night dragged on and on. Eventually it started to get bright outside. Fidler put out the lamp, opened the window, and stuck out her head. A mild wind was blowing. The sky was clear, and the last of the stars were just about visible. She felt tired, terribly tired, and she sat pensively on a chair by the window. The brightness of the new day brought a freshness and clarity into her confused thoughts. By the time she left her room that morning everything was already clear: She must leave!

She must get away from there, where her life had become so muddled, she must go away and once again become the person she used to be, with her silent longing, her silent suffering, and her silent dreams.

That very afternoon she went to see Dr. Vaynshteyn. He got a fright when he saw her face; she was pale and looked deadly serious.

"What's wrong? Are you ill? Sit down . . ." he said.

"I've come to say goodbye, Mr. Vaynshteyn. I'm leaving today. Only I need a few more rubles for a ticket. Can you lend it to me?"

"I don't understand; have a seat," and he brought her a chair. Fidler decided to be strict with him. During the night she had hated him, but now, feeling his kind, gentle eyes on her, she was once again reluctant to offend him and so she sat down.

"Well, tell me, what's wrong?"

"I need to go away, I'm finished; what's keeping me here?"

"Listen," he said, and his voice because earnest, without a hint of levity. "Listen, Lyuba, stay here, stay and be my wife, I love you . . ."

He took her hand. She thought for a while before she gently slipped her hand out of his grip and said: "No, Mr. Vaynshteyn, that won't be possible. You were wrong, I'm sorry."

She spoke these words clearly and distinctly, with pleasure and pride, feeling how each word made her heart freer and lighter. Dr. Vaynshteyn just wiped his forehead; his face had taken on a pained expression. He paced several times over the room and said, "Forgive me..."

As she left, he squeezed her hand tightly; the cold smile had returned to his face and he repeated, "Forgive me," this time without rancor.

A few days later Fidler was gone from Warsaw.

Two years passed. Dr. Vaynshteyn was now living in Switzerland. His father had died, leaving him a large inheritance that he did not know what to do with, and nor did he know what to do with himself. He had already forgotten all about Fidler. A coincidence, however, reminded him of her.

In the evenings he liked to walk by the lake for hours before coming home to sleep. One night he opened up the Russian newspaper, which brought daily news from a country that already seemed so foreign to him, and which he liked to read in bed just before going to sleep. There in the newspaper he came across a familiar name. He read:

Yesterday the murderer of General A. was hanged: the Jewess, Lyuba Fidler.

He did not sleep that night. For several days afterwards he felt numb, and at night he dreamed of bombs and carnage, of gallows and stiff human bodies shaking in the wind.

1907

47

Who Is to Blame?

... My roommate Finkelman is asleep. It's been barely a minute since he put out the lamp next to his bed, and he's already snoring. He had already dozed off a while ago, but mid-slumber it occurred to him that he was wasting oil, so he tore himself violently from his bed to extinguish the lamp. He's now lying completely in shadow: the light from my desk does not reach as far as the wall.

His sleep is never peaceful: he snores, he grimaces, his dark eyebrows twitch—he must dream a lot. But tonight I could almost swear that his snoring is swallowing many sighs. He's an altogether pitiful sight, with his small, huddled body and that pale, tormented face of his sticking out from under the blanket. His eyebrows wriggle, and he knits his brow. What is he dreaming about? About his wife? About his dead child? Or about a divorce followed by a new marriage with a dowry?

Somehow he has made a strange impression on me today.

I've been living in this room with him for three weeks now. When I moved in and became his roommate I was astonished by how animated he was. We had never met before. He was so energized and couldn't wait to show me everything—right down to the tiniest nail for hanging clothes—grabbing things from my hands and carrying them in an attempt to be helpful, nodding his head all the while. He was so passionate that I couldn't help myself and had to ask why he was going to so much trouble.

"It's no trouble! Leave it. Leave it," he said, helping me against my will.

He gesticulated wildly as he spoke and pulled back his lips to reveal his teeth; his eyes were gleeful and inquisitive. With that smile he clearly hoped to reassure me that his extraordinary helpfulness was on account of his good nature. But besides that grin there was something more to his gaze, as though he were waiting, eager to know if the smile had made the desired impression and if it was now safe to close his lips.

"Doing favors," he said, bounding a step closer with each word, "doing favors—why ever not, I enjoy doing favors. Here, here, my dear friend, hang your clothes here!" Then, seeing me open a drawer to put away my copied Russian lessons, he continued, "Not there! Look here, my dear friend." His face grew more serious. "That's *my* drawer, you see. I arranged it like that with the landlord—you can ask him if you like."

I removed the papers and was about to put them into my trunk when he grabbed them from my hand and opened his drawer again.

"See, *for you,* my dear friend, just *for you,* I'll let you keep them in my drawer. You know Russian?" he asked suddenly, noticing what was written on my papers.

"Yes, I do."

"Oh, wonderful, wonderful! You see, I'm learning Russian myself. My pronunciation is not very good. Will you speak to me in Russian? You'll teach me, won't you, my dear friend? Oh, wonderful! You'll teach me?"

He once again made the same face as before: he smiled, but this time his eyes contained a naïve pleading, like a child asking an adult for a penny.

Since then he has barely spoken a word of Yiddish to me. His Russian is bad; he makes a lot of mistakes and wants to use the time we spend together correcting those mistakes. After every correction, I hear: "Oh, *spasibo, spasibo!* Thank you, thank you! *Vi kharoshi gospodin!* You are a good gentleman!"

Generally, whether speaking to me or to someone else, he addresses everyone as "sir" or "*gnädiger Herr.*" When I told him that, in Russian, the formal pronoun is all the politeness one needs, he ignored me. He no doubt reasons that if you can do someone a favor by calling him *"gnädiger Herr"* then whyever not?

We sat down together at the table to smoke. Finkelman helped himself to one of my cigarettes and assured me he was only smoking for my sake. I later discovered that I wasn't the only one to benefit from such a favor. In fact, like all neurotics (Finkelman's face and movements are highly neurotic) he enjoys smoking very much but would never go as far as buying his own cigarettes; he is too stingy for that.

The landlord of the neighboring rooms came in to borrow a match, and I was startled when Finkelman sprang to his feet, deftly grabbed the matches from my hand, and proferred them to the landlord with the same expression and the same smile I mentioned before.

"A match?" he said eagerly, taking a little hop with each word. "A match, eh? Here you are! Take a few more, there you go! It's no trouble, it's no trouble at all!"

This was on Friday, and Finkelman, who makes a living as a Hebrew teacher, had already finished work for the day. He lay on his bed reading a couple of tattered pages from an old Russian newspaper. He explained that he'd found them in a shop where they were being used as wrapping paper, and since he was learning Russian and had a Russian dictionary, he'd bought the whole lot for three kopecks.

"Damn them anyway!" he said. "Trying to fleece people like that; you could buy a whole pound of wrapping paper for three kopecks. You see, my dear friend"—he shoved the pages into my hand—"you see, altogether it weighs no more than half a pound. Highway robbery!"

He accompanied those words with such a grimace that it was hard to look at him.

He lay there reading out loud, asking me the meaning of words every minute or so. The newspaper article was about economic statistics; he understood very little of it, and this seemed to trouble him.

I soon tired of explaining words to him. Each explanation required quite a bit of commentary, on top of which I was obliged to avoid using words that Finkelman might consider pretentious: he would sneer each time I used a word he'd never heard before. I noticed that he was actually quite clever; his faculties were well oiled from reading the Talmud, and he could easily get his head around complex things quickly and accurately. After each explanation he smiled and thanked me in his usual way: shaking his head, raising his eyebrows. But there was something catlike in his eyes, something false and exaggerated.

To make the work easier for myself, I suggested he read one of Dostoyevsky's books: *Crime and Punishment*, which I happened to have in my trunk. Finkelman leapt from his bed with great joy, grabbed my shoulders with both hands, and shook me in celebration, saying over and over: "*Spasibo, spasibo, vi kharoshi gospodin!*"

His arms and legs were trembling. He was so overcome that his whole body wriggled like a fish.

He didn't even let me get as far as the trunk; he grabbed the key from my hand, opened the trunk, and began rooting around inside. I was left standing there like a golem, like a block of wood, angry with myself. If memory serves, my whole mind was smothered in one thought: "What's he doing? He's rummaging through my things!" But I was in no mood to argue. He sat on the floor going through my possessions, flinging aside one book after another.

Once he set about reading Dostoyevsky, he again started asking questions. Almost every sentence required several minutes of discussion. I put on my coat and made for the door; Finkelman looked at me pleadingly.

"You're not leaving, are you?" he asked.

"I need to go."

"But look," he said tearfully, "the whole week I have no time to read, I'm busy from morning to night with ten lessons to teach. Stay here at home! What harm will it do you? You're a good gentleman, after all; where are you going?"

I had no intention of staying, and I could see that Finkelman resented it. He bit his lip like one who has been terribly wronged and is unable to defend himself. He regarded me with surprise and not a little regret, no doubt thinking: "What despicable people there are in the world; they could do you favors that wouldn't cost them a single penny, and yet they refuse!"

When I returned a few hours later Finkelman was still lying on the bed, deeply engrossed in his reading. He didn't even hear me come in. I'll be honest, I had not imagined for a moment that a book could interest him so much. There was a stern expression on his face, like Raskolnikov himself in mid-murder. You could tell that it wasn't his desire to learn Russian vocabulary spurring him on this time; the subject matter was quite different, and now his soul was engaged.

I sat down quietly by the table, and he let out a sudden loud sigh. Seeing that I had returned, he sprang out of bed and ran toward me. He couldn't speak; the book must have really gotten to him. He twisted up his lips as if wanting to smile, but something entirely different came out—I don't know what you would even call it.

This time he spoke in Yiddish: "Oh, he's a clever one!" he said, pointing a finger at the book on the bed. "A real clever bastard; what power he has! If only I could write like that!"

He had caught my interest.

"What would you do?" I asked.

"Ah, ah, if I could write like that, what do you think, my dear friend, I wouldn't be here, would I? How much could he earn from a book like that? Is he still alive? At least a few hundred rubles, I reckon. Oh, my dear friend, if I could write like that I'd immediately bring my young wife here to live with me; what do you think? She's beautiful, I tell you, a real gem ... prettier than all the others ..."

He then got into some crude talk, which I won't repeat here. So it seems he's a slave to his passions: he's stingy and prone to losing his temper over trifles, and he suffers a lot because of it.

From his careless words I learned that he has a wife in some small town in Lithuania—I don't remember which one—and that he wants a divorce because they haven't paid him the dowry. He loves his wife—she is quite beautiful according to him—but hates the father-in-law because he tricked him and hasn't given him a single kopeck of the three hundred rubles he'd promised. Finkelman says that he must divorce the wife and avenge himself on his father-in-law: let him do with her what he will.

I could see that it wasn't just about revenge; the missing three hundred rubles lay heavy on his heart. He also told me that he'd already had a child with her, but it had died. He never saw the child because he'd run away right after the wedding, once he had learned that his father-in-law was a complete pauper and was in no position to give him a single ruble. He showed up at the circumcision but didn't speak to anyone there; he just gave a name to the child and left. I can only imagine how the young mother must have wept. While he told me this story, I realized he was glad that the child had died: he almost let slip a *"slava bogu,"* a Russian "praise be to God," but caught himself mid-phrase and swallowed the *"bogu."* I know that he makes such mistakes because he's speaking in Russian: he has to concentrate to express his thoughts in a foreign language and so he forgets himself in the process. He was glad about the child's death for one very simple reason: it makes it easier to get a divorce.

I learned all of this three weeks ago, on Friday, when I moved in. Since then I haven't spoken to him at length. During the week he is busy from nine in the morning until ten at night; he teaches ten different students living on ten different streets. I'm rarely at home on Friday nights, and Finkelman is quite annoyed at me because of it. He likes to read on Fridays and wants me to sit with him all day, pronouncing Russian words. He genuinely believes that I'm a bad person, but what can I do?

It might be better for me to find somewhere else to live.

He sets off early in the mornings while I'm still asleep. In the evenings he comes home late, sighs a few times, and starts complaining about some of his students' parents who follow the Russian calendar, which is longer than the Jewish one, and other such things. He always finishes up by telling me the same story about a man who has owed him eight rubles for two months now, and how he, Finkelman, doesn't make a big deal of it because the man is poor.

That's Finkelman's version of events, at any rate. Who knows if it's the truth. But once he reaches that particular anecdote, I know his tirade is drawing to a close and he will soon eat dinner. Then I won't need to nod anymore—if I don't nod while he speaks he gets offended and shoots me such an evil look—with fury even—which I cannot abide. He's now much colder toward me than before, though he still asks me to explain Russian words and thanks me in that strange manner of his. In his heart he has already built up a great deal of animosity toward me.

You can tell from how he eats that he used to be a poor yeshiva student, accepting charitable meals at different houses each day. He stares at the bread for a long time before partaking, leaves nothing behind, and smacks his lips as if he had always found eating difficult, something he's spent a lot of time contemplating. I don't mean how to put food on the table—everyone thinks about that. I mean the act of eating itself: the transfer of food from the plate and into his mouth. Most people do that without thinking, but a yeshiva boy has to think and eat at the same time.

Once (it was ten days ago, if I'm not mistaken) he arrived home in an excellent mood. He was just about to place his hands on my shoulders but withdrew them, then he sat down and stared at me long and hard with an earnest, pleading expression.

"Why are you such a bad friend to me?" he asked.

I could tell that he wanted to confide something joyous, something happy, and was setting up the story; I assured him that I wasn't a bad friend to him.

"Then you're a good friend?" he asked, so delighted that he switched to Yiddish.

"You see! I knew from the moment I met you that you were a good person! I like you very much, my dear friend. Why don't you want to teach me Russian? You see," he said, taking out a booklet from the government savings bank and showing it to me, "praise God, ten rubles already! Ahh, just wait until I've saved a hundred rubles . . ."

"What will happen?" I asked.

"Ah! Oh! When I have a hundred rubles, I will go to America."

"What good is America to you?"

He glared at me, making a sour face and said: "You see, my friend, I have only today sent word home that I'm heading to America; if I abandon my wife she will be an *agunah*. She'll have no chance of getting a divorce then! But what fault of mine is it?"

I understood that really he did not want to go to America, but he was telling people, and trying to convince himself that he did, in order to threaten his wife into asking for a divorce. That's what he tells everyone, and he's starting to believe it himself. He's no stranger to lies: he tells a mountain of them, with his face, with his hands, and even with his heart. He is like a child.

It's a strange thing to say and yet it's true: when he lies I like him a lot more than when he tells the truth. It must be because he talks too openly, exposing his sullied heart. It's hard to bear, and in those moments I would gladly explain a thousand Russian words to him if only he would start telling a few lies, so that his face should become more tolerable.

That night he was nothing but kind to me; he grabbed hold of me by the shoulders a couple of times and shook me, peppering the conversation with *"Vi kharoshi gospodin."*

He told me how he had been tricked into going home six months ago. They sent him a telegram saying that his mother had died. Seeing his wife again had moved him to pity, and so he had stayed with her for a few days. He had intended to get his three hundred rubles, but the father-in-law must have been hard up, because Finkelman returned to Warsaw empty-handed.

"You know, my dear friend," he said to me, stretched out on the bed, his face twisted up in great pleasure—his nose seemed even pointier than usual—"you know I was afraid . . . that there might be some consequence from me being at home. If you understand what I mean . . . a new child is the last thing I need! That much I'm sure of. You see? Tell me, my dear friend, if something were wrong she would write to me, wouldn't she? Tell me, dear friend!"

He was looking for assurance that his wife was not pregnant.

"What do you think?" he badgered me, excitement entering his eyes. "What do you think? A fine little wife, such pinchable cheeks, I tell you, they are simply—aah!"

We talked for a long time. I discovered that he had recently become an atheist; he had even stopped praying. He spoke about his abandoned faith with resentment, cursing, repeating that he had been swindled. On that last point he was incessant, repeating the word *"obmanshik"* again and again. He also told me that the previous winter, when he had still been observant, he had been unable to accept an early morning lesson on account of having to pray in the mornings, and he was very angry about it. He worked out that over time he would have earned twenty-four rubles, and today, added to the fifty rubles he had in his savings book, he would have had seventy-four rubles.

When I came home at eight o'clock this evening, I was surprised to see that Finkelman was already home. I could see on his face that something was wrong; he was so distracted he didn't even return my "good evening."

He sat by the table, biting his lips, shifting nervously around in his chair. He was turning a postcard over in his hands. He glared at me every now and then, and I saw torment in his eyes, a great sorrow. He had been crying, and there were still tears in his eyes.

"What's wrong, Finkelman?" I asked.

He pretended not to hear, then tried to change the subject: "How are you, my dear friend?"

But his words did not come out clearly. The grief caught in his throat and we both knew that he was on the verge of tears.

"God damn it!" He slammed his fist on the table, took out his purse, counted out some small change, and ran off down the stairs. A few seconds later he was back, out of breath: he must have run the whole way. He held in his hand a message-reply card, which he had just bought downstairs.

He sat down at the table, saying nothing, and filled in the addresses on the card: on one half he inscribed the destination, and of course his own on the other.

Then he took the other postcard out of his jacket pocket and read it with great intent, one line, one word at a time. He sighed heavily and began writing. He wrote furiously, like someone unloading a heavy burden, and his face changed with each line. Writing seemed to bring him some relief.

He held the finished card up to the lamp to dry for quite some time, shaking it back and forth. Only afterward did he set it down on the table, fixing it with an expression that I find difficult to describe.

I remember now, at my father's funeral, when I was still a boy and my father was already lying in the ground, the shammes came to us children and tore a patch from each of our garments. I recall my youngest brother taking the torn patch in his hands and turning it over, over and over, examining it from all sides. He'd stared at that patch just as Finkelman had stared at that card a few hours ago, with a deep sadness mixed with a little bewilderment: "What does this rent garment have to do with anything?"

He stared at the card a little longer. Then he slowly walked over to his trunk and took out a bundle of letters, including several message-reply cards. He read over a few of the letters, then added the postcard he had just written to the pile and put them all back into the trunk.

He had already grown much calmer. The card he had received was still lying face down on the table.

"Read it, my friend!"

This is what it said (I have it here in front of me):

My dear, loyal husband, Yankev Yehuda (long may you live),
     Firstly, I write to you in good health and wish to always hear the same from you, *Omeyn selo.*
     Secondly, I'm writing to say that I no longer have the energy to cry, and I didn't have the money for a postcard. I borrowed the money for this one. My dear husband, how have I failed you?
     When I come to Warsaw I will eat bread and salt, and I will wash floors. And I beg you, write and tell me I should come, and send me the travel costs. God will send you fortune through me. This is already the fifth postcard I'm sending you, and I haven't received a reply. May God bring you aid on my

behalf. Have pity on me and my young years. *Omeyn selo.*
    Your wife, who hopes to see you,
    Zelda Finkelman

On the side had been added in tiny handwriting:

They have thrown us out of the house. Write that I should come. I will find the money. I don't know what to do! Father has gone away, and I'm sleeping at Rokhl-Khane's.

When I had finished reading, he fixed me long and hard with his eyes and I understood that he was waiting to hear my verdict. He was racked with guilt.

"Bring her to Warsaw," I said. "What would cost you more?"

But he did not let me finish.

"What? Without a penny from her side of the family? Three hundred rubles she promised me! Why did she have to swindle me? I studied in Lomzhe for eight years—eight years!" He thumped the table twice with his fist. "I slept on the hard benches and fasted, and they beat me! Now I ask you: for what? An arranged marriage without a penny! I suffered and toiled for eight years and should marry without a penny! Is it my fault if he has a daughter? Well, tell me, what fault is it of mine? That he has a daughter? Is it my fault?"

"But of course it's not her fault either, is it?" I ventured.

Finkelman grabbed his wife's postcard from my hands. I saw that he was once again distressed. He began reading the postcard again but suddenly burst into tears: "What fault is it of mine?"

He went over to his chest, taking out the packet of letters that he had only just put in.

"Look," he said passing them to me, "see for yourself: Ten letters I've written to her, telling her to come! Message-reply cards—return postage prepaid!—so she can write back and tell me when I should expect her. There they are, unsent . . . did you think I didn't know that I wouldn't send today's letter either? I knew, I could have just sent an old letter! I knew . . . Here, read!"

I remember the following words from his postcard:

"My dear soul, I have sinned against you, my dear life, come soon for God's sake, I miss you terribly, I cannot live without you," and other such words.

"Those have cost me more than fifty kopecks, those letters."

He had already calmed down and was about to eat dinner.

"I know it's a waste of money, and it distresses me, my friend, that I have to waste money for that, you understand—I have to spend money . . . Well, tell me yourself, what do they want from me? What do I owe *them*?"

I didn't answer him, because I understood that it was a waste of time. He was now entirely calm, scrutinizing his bread and placing each piece into his mouth with the sweet satisfaction of a long-awaited desire at last fulfilled. It wasn't long before he got undressed and went to bed.

He didn't go to his lessons today. The maid told me that she had seen him pacing around the room for hours, gibbering to himself like a madman.

Now he's asleep, and snoring loudly. He wrinkles up his brow and smacks his lips . . . What's he dreaming about? About his wife with the nice cheeks, which are so "aah" for him to pinch? And what does his wife dream about, poor thing, an unwanted guest at her neighbor's place, sleeping on the floor? Does she sigh in her sleep? Does she beg for pity from that husband of hers, and cry for help: "But it's not my fault!"

If I wanted to, I could walk over to Finkelman right now, grab him by the neck, and strangle him with my own hands until his tongue stuck out. I imagine that, as with any great transgression, it must be quite satisfying to spit on the outstretched tongue of a man as his face writhes in the throes of death.

And now I think back to what he looked like when he was crying and clapping his chest: "What fault is it of mine?" He must really have suffered a lot of hunger, want, and shame during those eight years at the yeshiva, he must have gone hungry more than once and been without anywhere to sleep many times, and he must have borne it all with a bent back, put up with everything, and in his mind there was only one, lone happy dream: a wife with a dowry. In his fantasy he kissed that wife for eight whole years, eight long years he counted that dowry and fantasized about the things he would do with it . . . and really, I begin to wonder, who's really to blame? Is it him, his bad soul, his great troubles, or that damned yeshiva of his? And what do I mean when I say *his soul*?

The lamp seems to be going out.

1901

In a Hasidic House

I found a job not long after I arrived in Warsaw. My boss was a Hasidic Jew, and I worked at his house drawing up documents, doing his accounts, and giving bookkeeping lessons to his son, an arrogant youth with a gold watch. He never said a word during the lessons, just looked off to the side with a face like a general listening to a report, and whenever I pointed out his mistakes he would glower at me with his eyes full of hate before storming off. Making small talk with a Litvak such as myself, a mere clerk, was beneath him. Of course the feeling was quite mutual, and I looked down on him and my boss as I would on wild fanatics.

I had just recently arrived from Lithuania with a head full of European ideas and "enlightenment," and the Warsaw Hasidim with their habits and that accent, where they draw out their words in a sort of singsong, seemed so peculiar and foreign to me; I couldn't have imagined anything more outlandish.

My boss worked as a contractor with the railways and was rarely at home. He was always in a hurry; barely in the door for lunch, he would cast aside his walking stick and start complaining that his food wasn't ready yet. And that mumbling of his: even though I heard it every day, I still couldn't understand him clearly. I could never tell where one word ended and the next began. I just saw how his long, black beard shook, his mustache trembled, and from his darkly overgrown mouth there came a low growling, from which I could only make out the words: "Lunch . . . lunch . . . never . . ." and the

61

monologue would end with the extended lament: "I've no tiiiime!"

Between one dish and the next he would suddenly stand up and empty his pockets onto the table before heading out the door. It was up to me to sort through the scraps of paper on which he had written down the sums of money that he'd paid his workers, along with various receipts, promissory notes, and so on. Everything was all crumpled up, and it took me ages to straighten things out, putting the papers in order and making a note of them in the ledger.

In the absence of any clear instructions, I was obliged to figure out what my job consisted of by myself. He spoke so quickly and with such a drawl, gesticulating so wildly that I didn't so much listen to him as observe him.

"And wee Isaac, eh?" he said, half swallowing his words. "He's learning, our Isaac? He's learning? Is he?"

But he always returned to his food before waiting to hear how his son was getting on. His wife, a tall, attractive older woman with clever eyes and an odd smile, usually called him over just as he was about to leave. Wiping away the noodles or bread crumbs that had found their way into his beard, she would ask him for money. He'd then lose his temper, and of his mumbled tirade I would only catch the fragments—"again . . . again . . . money . . . money . . ."—before these ramblings finally culminated, in the plaintive melody of a Talmudic question, with the words: "What do you need money for?"

His wife, of course, had no difficulty understanding his speech despite paying very little attention to what he said. She'd do up the last button on his jacket and look straight into his eyes, and her mischievous expression seemed to have an effect on him.

She would ask him again softly, and this time he would give her a few coins, his hairy face and jittery little eyes showing signs of joy and happiness at odds with his hurried bearing. Aside from business and lucre, my boss apparently also loved his wife.

It was hard to say whether she loved him or not. I never got the chance to ask her about it, even though we often discussed all sorts of things. When no one else was home she would sit down next to me at my worktable and strike up a conversation. She spoke about everything, and always in the same tone. She was curious about me: why wasn't I married? Was I in love with some girl, or had I never thought about marriage at all? She was attentive and wanted to hear what I had to say.

"I've heard about old bachelors . . . I don't understand it myself," she said with a smile.

She also spoke Yiddish with a Warsaw accent, but the singsong intonation and drawl that made the men sound so ridiculous was much more suited to the fairer sex. She had a very pleasant voice, weary, sad, and full of yearning. I told her that getting married was not so easy. Only the lofty, noble, and mighty feeling that we call *love* can join two souls together for a lifetime. I held forth with the enthusiasm that only a young man of twenty-two could have for talking about love. She heard me out, enviously, never breaking eye contact, and it was hard for me to bear her cold, mocking gaze. She listened strictly out of courtesy, as one listens to a know-it-all child expounding on well-worn topics. I asked myself if this slim, pretty woman in the wig had already forgotten the feeling of love that I had only read about in books.

I stopped talking and went back to work, but the next day and the day after that she joined me again for a chat. She invariably wanted to talk about the same things, and she certainly did not talk like a Hasidic wife; she spoke dispassionately, and with that kind of irony that is particular to very beautiful women past their prime, who do not doubt themselves or their beauty. Eventually I couldn't help myself and had to ask:

"Why do you wear a wig?"

She was visibly thrown by the question, losing some of the detached, poker-faced calm that had irritated me. She blushed under her wig.

"Trust me," she said in a quiet, shocked voice, "it's not such a big thing: what's the problem? You're not a real person if you wear a wig? You think I'm doing it for my benefit? What can one do, I have children . . . a husband . . ."

This time she was the one who ended the conversation, and she ignored me for several days.

Later, when my question had been all but forgotten, we resumed our long conversations. She wasn't as backward as I had thought. She liked to talk about every topic under the sun, but I had the feeling she wasn't really interested in anything I had to say.

Once or twice a week, a young, clean-shaven man of about thirty, who always wore a short jacket, visited after lunch. I later learned that he was her cousin, a rich man with whom my boss had some sort of business. He always asked the same question:

"How are things? Is Osher home? No? That's a shame."

He never removed his hat before sitting down at the table. Madame Pernberg—Pernberg was my boss's name—sat across from him. They spoke in low voices, drinking tea and glancing at me occasionally. Then my boss's wife got dressed and they went off together. Apart from that, everything in the house was strictly Hasidic: the boy was rarely without his prayer shawl and wore a yarmulke under his silk hat. Khanele, the daughter, would hide whenever a strange man came to the house, and they did not trust the cook to salt the meat or to open up a chicken. My boss often went to see the Rebbe. On one occasion the boy took the liberty of wearing a modern shirt with an ironed collar and got a good scolding from his father for doing so. Even his mother shouted at him, admittedly a little halfheartedly and only for the sake of appearances, but the boy never tried anything like it again.

II

Khanele was still a young girl of about seventeen or eighteen. She had inherited her mother's beauty, but her face was softer and hadn't lost the fresh color of budding youth. Her height, her solidly built body, her dark, well-defined eyebrows, and her full, passionate lips reminded me of her mother, but there was no sign of the smile that sparkled in her mother's eyes. In fact, I had no idea what her eyes looked like; I didn't exchange a single word with her the whole three months. As soon as I entered a room she would leave. I only saw her when she passed through, and even then only in profile. By the time

I'd raised my eyes to look at her she had already disappeared through a door. She intrigued me, and I felt a sort of pity for her. A young girl in bloom, full of life and beauty, who moves with such light, lovely grace, with so much potential for spreading fresh, vital happiness everywhere around her. Such a young creature, who finds herself so cut off from other people, sitting locked up all day, never seeing anybody, flowering and then withering in the darkness—why? For what? What does she do all day? What goes through her young mind? I'm not sure if she noticed my existence; she never cast so much as a cursory glance in my direction. She walked through the house with straight, measured steps, her gaze always fixed on her destination, and I could only catch the briefest glimpse of that pretty body slipping past and disappearing. It bothered me sometimes. Was it because I was a Litvak? A clerk? Am I not even worth looking at? Her proud gait, the calm, measured steps and her self-assured expression did not allow the possibility that she was just a shy, stupid girl, too ashamed to make eye contact. She remained a puzzle to me.

Each day I arrived at work with the hope that I would discover something new about her, that I might get to know her, and every day I returned home disappointed, burdened by a mystery that always remained as enigmatic as it ever had.

I remember waiting for her impatiently while I sat working. I knew she was right there in the next room, and I kept wondering whether the door would open or not. Then, when I'd already lost patience and had gone back to my books, the door would open and in she'd come, walking slowly and calmly, before disappearing into the kitchen. I sat there, ashamed and unsatisfied, as though I had been left speechless by an insult. I was annoyed, and yet I missed her and longed for her to come back. The slightest noise from the direction of the door made my heart race. I had never even heard her voice— how does she speak? Loudly or softly, slowly or quickly? I exhausted myself trying to imagine how her voice and laugh would sound. Ten times a day I conceived of her voice differently; I once dreamed that she spoke sternly, irritably, like those people who always feel the need to separate themselves from life and enjoyment. Another time I dreamed that her voice was full of softness, goodness, and repressed feelings, or even that she spoke with a smile, lively and fast, and I imagined how her lips—her lovely, full, red lips—moved as she spoke ...

But my fantasies could not satisfy me, and with each passing day she obsessed me more and more. It was only after two months of working in the house that I finally heard her laugh. I happened upon her in the room with another girl, who must have just told her something amusing because she was laughing loudly. She leaned against her friend's shoulder as she laughed, her white teeth shining. But then she noticed me and stopped. Her face went blank, losing all expression, and she walked straight into the next room with the other girl. That sound echoed in my ears long after she had left, and for the rest of the day I found it hard to concentrate on my work, making numerous mistakes in my calculations.

I tormented myself trying to recall that smile in all its detail; I felt like a detective who holds in his hands some objective evidence with which he seeks to reach the *truth*. Her laugh, as I've already mentioned, was a joyful and happy one, not a nervous one. I tried in vain to find in it the tiniest hint of sorrow, of the smothered youth of a Hasidic daughter. One month went by after another. My work suffered. I would stand at the wall and try to overhear Khanele in the next room. But the wall was too thick, or Khanele spoke quietly on purpose—either way I heard nothing. I felt as though Khanele had taken over my mind, leaving me unable to think about anything else. I started frittering away all my hard-earned money on new clothes, wondering constantly whether Khanele would like my new hat or my new tie, wondering if they would make me more handsome and respectable. I went without lunch, without other important things; buying here a pin, there a tie, even though I had never in my life played the dandy or paid much attention to sartorial matters. It was as though I had become a new man. I remember sitting there on one occasion and realizing that my tie was crooked. It would never have bothered me before, but this time I felt a sudden shock and was livid as though I'd done something terrible. Why? Because Khanele could have walked in at that very moment and seen me in such a state, with a crooked tie, and ridiculed me! I drifted alone through the street, daydreaming. My fantasies carried me far away and I felt good, carefree, and lighthearted. Whole speeches arranged themselves in my mind . . . I explained to Khanele what a woman is, what a real life is, that she was living a lie, that she was blind. In my head I spoke to her with loving words, and I saw how her face changed, how her eyes sparkled. As she listened she threw me a look that was shy, yet passionate. "Good, pious soul," I mumbled to myself. It sometimes happened that, in the middle of my reveries, I'd recall her laugh, and my fantasies would be interrupted. That laugh derailed my thoughts, like a false note in a beautiful motif, and I was left feeling unsettled. But everything went on just as before in the house. The boss's wife still spoke with me, but I answered indifferently, without much emotion. I wasn't interested in what she was talking about, and she wasn't inclined to talk about the things that would really have interested me, about which she could have told me a great deal. I was afraid to bring up her daughter. I got the impression that there was something going on between mother and daughter. During my first month on the job, Khanele was often in the room where I worked, and I made an observation. Khanele was standing by the sideboard, looking for something, or pretending to look for something. Her mother came in, glancing first at me, then at Khanele, who seemed—or so I thought—to be deliberately ignoring her. She went over to the cupboard and asked her daughter what she was looking for. Khanele said something I could not hear and then left the room, followed by her mother. From that moment on Khanele kept her distance from me.

But once some time had passed she began to appear more often, sometimes even glancing in my direction. Such glances gave me enough material to think about for a whole day, consoling me, inspiring hope. But I managed to sabotage my own contentment. I once got into a conversation with the boy. He was in a reasonably good mood, having just received a new gift from his future father-in-law, a silver cigar case: the gilding was "quite special," the lock was "something else," and so on.

"And is your fiancée pretty?" I asked.

The question caught him off guard. He glared at me, bewildered, and said, "Of course! What did you expect? That I wouldn't have a pretty fiancée?" He glanced around to see if anyone was listening. He made me swear not to breathe a word to anyone and then told me how, every Saturday, he likes to loiter outside a particular house his fiancée frequents, and where he sees her.

"And what do you two talk about?"

"She doesn't know who I am," he answered casually. "When she walks past I bow down, like this."

"And what does she think?"

"Didn't you hear? She doesn't know who I am! Oh, one time she blushed!"

He started to laugh but was suddenly shocked by his own words. I figured that the whole story was a product of his imagination. That he wouldn't risk spying on his fiancée and that the whole thing was for my benefit, to show off.

"You won't tell anyone, right? Look, please don't say anything," he said firmly, fiddling with his cigar case.

I took advantage of his confusion and began inquiring about his sister.

"You have a nice sister," I attempted to flatter him. "A pretty girl ... rare."

"Khanele? Ha! She's a nobody; my fiancée is much prettier!"

As foolish as it sounds, I have to admit that I was annoyed, and I had to resist telling him he had no idea what he was talking about.

"What does she do all day?" I inquired.

"My fiancée?"

"No, your sister Khanele."

My tone must have awakened his suspicion, or he may have been offended that I was speaking about Khanele instead of about his fiancée. He answered reluctantly:

"What should she do? How should I know? You want to know everything?"

He must have mentioned our conversation to someone, because

afterward the atmosphere in the house was quite different. Khanele stopped appearing altogether. The boss's wife didn't talk to me anymore, instead looking at me askance while my boss began dropping hints that maybe I should start looking for a new job.

And what about Khanele? The poor thing! I had almost certainly caused her some grief, and for what? If only I could at least speak to her, to apologize, but how?

I came to work one morning to find the house empty. I was distracted and tired, having slept very badly. Khanele was in the kitchen, and my heart beat so impatiently that the pen trembled in my hand. I could feel her youth and freshness, her slim body and her soft gaze from the other side of the wall. Everything in me was drawn toward the next room, but that cold, unmoving wall stood mutely between us like a terrible force. My gaze fell upon the mirror; I appeared pale and strangely weak and helpless. I was taken aback by my own reflection. Suddenly the door opened and Khanele, holding a key in her hand, strode straight toward me. I rose from my chair in shock. She approached, calmly laid the key down on the table, and said, "Daddy told me to ask you to take two promissory notes to the bank."

I wanted to say something, but my heart was pounding, and she slipped out again, quietly and calmly before I had a chance.

Why didn't I talk to her? I cursed myself, biting my lip in anger. But even in my imagination it was hard to think of something to say. What could I have said to her, a pious, Hasidic daughter? How was our conversation supposed to begin? It was only later that evening that I realized she'd put the key down on the table, rather than hand it to me directly. That was obviously some Hasidic custom. I could have asked, with a friendly smile and a gentle voice, why she'd put the key down on the table and not into my hand. What an excellent question! But wisdom cannot be rushed: as with all brilliant afterthoughts, the question only occurred to me later in the evening as I was walking through the streets. Back there in the room, I'd been paralyzed with terror.

III

A few days later, the boy had news for me. "You know something, teacher?" he said. "You won't be here for much longer; Daddy's hired someone else."

"Why?" I asked, holding back the rage toward that loathsome boy that had been building up inside me over the last few days.

"How would I know?" he answered in a singsong, scowling fiercely. "Mother says that we can't keep a young man like you here; you could corrupt the whole house. You think I don't know, eh? I know! You thought you'd get away with it . . ."

"What do you know?" I shouted.

"Don't try to fool me, please; I'm smarter than you—even if you are a Litvak—mark my words . . ."

As with all boys his age, he thought it was terribly clever to talk about girls and make dirty jokes, and he'd disliked me for a while now because I didn't like getting dragged into conversations with him about such topics. I tried in vain to glean from him what manner of calumny had been spread about me. He answered with a smile, avoiding clear responses. I remarked that the situation itself did not interest him in the slightest; he just wanted to show me how clever he was with his jokes. I flew into a rage.

"To hell with you and your jokes, barbarian!" I shouted. "What kind of person are you? If you want to learn, then learn. If not, don't and leave me in peace!"

He scowled at me.

"Look at this! A Litvak losing his temper? You think you're some sort of aristocrat or something? You're nobody, to hell with you! What are you even doing here? You think you're so *enlightened*, with your worn-out shoes and ripped trousers!"

I remember raising my hand—who knows what I would have done to him—but then my gaze fell reluctantly upon my shoes; they were indeed worn out.

I lowered my hand, my eyes filling with tears. The room and everything in it heaved and trembled around me. Tired, weary, and breathless, I collapsed on the chair. The boy left. I stood up and looked at my shoes again, completely disheveled! I said to myself, but what did he have against my trousers? "What does he have against my trousers?" I repeated, not knowing why it made me so angry. In my rage I wanted only one thing: to drag the boy back in by the hair and show him that my trousers were intact—no holes, not a single stain—that he was a liar, simply a liar with no right to say such things. A few moments later his mother entered. Without looking at me, she said, "What was all that with my little Isaac? Did you have a fight? He's only a child, you know. What do you want from him?"

That son of hers had a neck on him, and a pair of broad shoulders like an athlete; I held my tongue.

"I'll tell you the truth," she continued, but I could no longer stand the breezy tone she took with me. Her speech, her mannerisms, her whole being—it all seemed so false now, so unnatural, that I did not understand how I'd managed to remain calm up to this point. I sternly asked her what they wanted from me, what sort of slander had they spread about me, and I rose threateningly to my feet, ready to throw a chair at her head.

"You see that! Getting angry! A Litvak will always be a Litvak. What have we ever done to you? Did you sign a contract saying we would keep you here forever? Please, is there any need to get so angry when we are behaving like decent people? I ask you, you're something of an educated young man . . ."

I couldn't listen to another word; putting on my coat, I prepared to leave. As I did, the door to the other room opened, and there was Khanele.

If you have ever woken up from a long, torturous nightmare to find that, in fact, you are safe at home in your own bed in snow-white sheets, surrounded by your nearest and dearest, awake or asleep, the morning sun shining fresh and cheerful outside, and you feel doubly happy after the heavy feelings of before—then you can imagine how I felt in the moment the door opened: my rage suddenly disappeared. I stood there, mesmerized, looking at that sweet face in the next room. I can still picture those few loose strands of hair that had fallen in front of her eyes; even the image of the blue flowers on her blouse is still burned into my brain. She stared at me, and her eyes— God knows how you'd describe the emotions they expressed! There are looks in which you lose your heart, your feelings, and your entire self, as if in an endless void. My hostility toward the boy, the mother's hypocrisy, my bruised ego, the worn out shoes: all of it floated away and vanished. I couldn't take my eyes off her; I stood and stared. It was a strange scene: me standing there peering toward the door, Khanele looking at me, and her mother watching both of us. No one said a word or moved an inch, as if we were all waiting to see what would happen next. But then I noticed a smile on Mrs. Pernberg's face, that cold ironic smile that could cool down the hottest heart. She smiled, and I was sure that she was jealous of her own daughter; indignity was written on her face.

"Are you waiting for money?" she exclaimed. "Please come back tomorrow and you'll be paid for the month."

The word *money* was the last straw for me. I said good day and left. Khanele remained utterly still; I could feel her gaze on my back. My heart was seized with a terrible pain as I crossed the threshold. I closed the door behind me *forever*. I thought, I'll never see Khanele again. When I bumped into the boy in the yard, I avoided his gaze, looking down at the ground. I imagined he would stick out his tongue at me if I looked at him, and really why shouldn't he? I'm a Litvak after all, a clerk whom one makes use of and chases away as one desires, whereas he is a wealthy boy with a gold watch and a silver cigar case, a rich father with a wealthy home always open to him, and a beautiful, beautiful sister! I begrudged him the latter most of all.

IV

The period that followed was a difficult one. The days and nights stretched out interminably. I slept poorly at night, and by day I wandered the streets, thinking about God knows what. Inevitably my mind returned to Khanele. There was a constant nagging and tearing in my heart that did not stop for even a minute. A melancholy like a dark fog had descended upon me, and I saw everything through that fog. I grew lazy and careless; I stopped worrying about my crooked tie. I didn't bother looking for a new job and had no idea what lay ahead.

It was autumn and rain poured from the heavens. The streets were wet, the sky was gloomy, and a cold wind blew. The gray sky looked as if it was covered in mold. Even the houses looked sad. The cobblestones seemed to weep. I had the impression that I too was a piece of loose stone, a lump of unneeded material, alone in the big city.

I was agitated; my nerves were like a taut string. Every noise, every glance left me utterly distressed. I could have gone to my former boss's home to pick up my final wages, but I kept putting it off from one day to the next. That would be the last chance. I was afraid to show my face there. To pass the time during my sleepless nights I started writing an article, with the intention of getting it published. The article was called "The Status of Hasidic Daughters in Poland." I don't clearly remember the contents of the article, but I do remember that I wrote it in the tone of *The Book of Lamentations*, full of sadness. Although it was about Hasidic daughters in general, in my mind I pictured the situation of one daughter in particular, Khanele. I depicted her life as the wilting of the best and brightest days of youth; how unhappy she was! As I wrote, I somehow failed to notice that I had no interest in "the status of Hasidic daughters in Poland," that I was just pouring out my overfilled heart onto the paper, which kindly humored me with rapt indulgence.

Suddenly, as I was writing, I felt a twinge in my heart followed by a constriction in my throat, and I burst into tears. This was unusual for me; the emotion seemed to be coming from someone else. I sobbed and was powerless to stop. I cried so loudly that my landlady, who lived in the front room, rushed in, holding her wig in her hand.

"What's wrong with you, young man?" she exclaimed. "Oh! Let me get you a cloth. You must go to the doctor." Hearing the cries of the wigless old woman, I somehow had the urge to laugh, but instead I began to cry even louder. The commotion attracted the attention of her husband, who came in followed by the maid and their two young children, who also started to cry. I was in a dreadful state and struggled with all my energy to pull myself together, but the more I tried, the more I sobbed.

"I'm okay, it's nothing really," I struggled to say. It felt like I was shouting, but my voice was swallowed up in my tears. Eventually I managed to calm myself just enough to put my landlady at ease. They lingered around for what seemed like forever until I finally convinced them to go back to bed.

As I reread what I had written, the tears returned. But now I cried differently: quietly, calmly, feeling relief. I read the article word by word, and it was as though someone else was reading it to me, that I was just a vessel. I was ashamed to think that I'd intended to have the article published. I wanted to expose my heart to anyone and everyone. I wanted their sympathy, or, failing that, their scorn.

As I wandered the streets one evening, I was sure my sadness would suffocate me. Back home in my small village the first snows used to cheer me up, filling me with a pleasant, calm feeling. But here in the big city the snow only added to my melancholy, reminding me of the long winter in a foreign city among strangers, in my new, unfamiliar life. The snow continued to fall, and soon it was trodden underfoot. I dragged my feet through the slush, not paying attention to where I was going. I had barely slept the previous night, and here I was with yet another long, dark, cold night ahead of me. What can one do with oneself? How can one run from one's own heart? I still had some money on me, so I headed toward Theater Square and bought a ticket for the cheap seats on the fourth floor. I handed my coat and wet hat to the doorman, took a lorgnette, and went to find my seat. It was hard to see what was happening on stage from up there in the fourth row of the fourth floor. People were shoving each other, creeping along the bench, and hanging from columns. I sat quietly and didn't even use my lorgnette. It disgusted me to look at the hundreds of people in the lower levels, all dressed up, well-fed, and satisfied—their hearts devoid of any emotion—who had come to while away the time, staring blankly at the stage so they would have something to talk about later. I would have preferred to see pale, eager faces, but all was calm, as if the whole world were really just a wedding, and there was no yearning or unhappiness at all. To this day, I stand by my opinion that only those who suffer should be allowed to listen to music; people for whom life is hard to bear, who need to forget themselves for a while. To listen to music, as an idle pastime, like playing cards or spreading gossip, is a boorish sin. Those who still have a spark of hope in their lives, or a crumb of will, do not need music. And if the great, world-famous musicians followed their consciences instead of their pockets, they would not give concerts in theaters for crowds of happy, healthy people but instead by the beds of the dying, of those who have not lost faith in their unhappiness, dying of dread and fright—but anyway, I'm digressing.

The orchestra started to play before the lights were dimmed in the theater. The audience moved as one, crawling over each other's heads. I sat and waited. Gradually things calmed down. The pure tones wafted up from below and took over, silencing the noise and murmurs. The motif was soft at first, leisurely and complacent, before giving way to a sort of sighing sound, like a cord snapping inside of a soul. The whole motif changed: stifled tears and muzzled sighs struggled to free themselves, but they were hindered by a powerful force that held them back, suppressing them until they once again tried to tear themselves away, more quietly this time, less hopeful than before. The music continued to grow quieter, weaker. The lights went down and the curtains came up.

I did not know what was happening onstage; my eyes dropped shut and my brain was engulfed in a sort of haze, penetrated only by fragments of thoughts and disjointed images. I could no longer tell if the players were singing or acting. The music poured into me, touching my heart and remaking it anew: sadness turned to happiness; pain to joy. There was an incredible sense of holiness, and I felt infinitely lighter and free. The first act had come to an end; the theater resounding with applause. Blinded by the light, I sighed deeply and looked around. The fourth floor was less crowded now; people had already started making their way out into the corridor. Remembering my lorgnette I began observing the audience, and on the second floor balcony opposite I noticed a familiar female face. She was sitting with a gentleman, deep in conversation. I couldn't believe my eyes: she looked remarkably like Khanele, the same forehead, and the same eyes with the well-defined, rounded eyebrows. I had difficulty making out the other details of her face; she was moving around too much, speaking and laughing. What could she be doing here in the theater? Khanele, a Hasidic daughter, who had not wanted to say a word to an unknown young man like me, who was ashamed even to make eye contact! And what would her parents say?

But at that moment she noticed that she was being watched. Her face became suddenly still, and there was no doubt about it—it was her, the calm, pious, and shy Khanele! It was all I could do not to scream out in surprise. The first thought that struck my mind was that I had been mistaken, my ego had tricked me: she was not shy, it wasn't out of modesty that she'd avoided talking to me for months, it was because I disgusted her: she couldn't stand me—it was as simple as that! I ground my teeth, filled with self-loathing. I was incensed at my misplaced pity for her, at my constant yearning, and especially at her, the Hasidic daughter.

The lights in the theater had long since dimmed, but I no longer had any interest in the music. I sat there, my hands clenched in one single fist, and I thought: where does she get the nerve to go to the theater with a strange man? How could a Hasidic daughter do that? How could she be so false? In that moment, her father would have been faster in forgiving her these transgressions than I was.

Luckily the second act was short. I was impatient to confront her—that was exactly what I intended to do. I didn't have to wait long; Khanele soon came out into the corridor, and next to her was a young man, impeccably dressed, clean-shaven with an impressive mustache. She saw me immediately, and her face twisted into a strange frown. I suddenly felt sorry for her and wished I could have hidden away. The moment passed; a few seconds later her face was once again calm. She said something to the young man and started walking toward me, slowly, calmly, as if everything was normal.

"Ah, Panie K.," she said, extending her hand. "You're here too? How are things?"

My legs trembled. I was afraid that I might turn hysterical at any moment. I didn't even think to shake her hand; I just stood there like a wall. She took back her outstretched hand and made as if to leave.

"Khanele," I managed to blurt out, grabbing her by the hand. She released herself from my grip, looked at me, and said, "Leave me alone, please . . . it's unseemly."

"Khanele . . ." I mumbled again, not knowing what to say. The young man was standing to one side, fiddling with his mustache and regarding us coldly.

"I have no time," she said, justifying herself. "I have to go home. You understand, don't you? The second act has only just finished . . ."

She again made as if to leave, and I once again felt as though I were losing her forever.

"Will I never see you again?" I asked, almost shouting.

"What?" she said with a smile, with her mother's smile. "I don't let people look at me? Do you need to tell me something?" she asked in a serious voice, looking me inquisitively in the eyes.

"Yes, I need to see you, I must see you . . ."

She seemed embarrassed, unable to respond. She returned to her escort, and they exchanged whispers. I saw him taking out his purse and showing her that he had money. What did it all mean? She came back over to me.

"If you want, you may see me tomorrow at seven in the evening," she said.

She named the street and the address, then walked away.

I left the theater right then, and my head started to clear. I recalled that laugh of hers. No! She wasn't a kosher, pious soul, as I had thought. It was obvious that she had plenty of experience talking to young men—that was clear from how calmly she had just greeted me. She'd been deliberately pretending to be shy with me so as to avoid all suspicions, and I had been completely taken in.

V

She was not even a minute late. At exactly seven o'clock she arrived with quick, easy steps. She spotted me immediately and gave me her hand: "Oh! Of course, I forgot!" she said playfully, trying to take back her hand. "I forgot that you don't shake hands with women, because you're so religious, right?"

But I refused to let go of her; after everything I had put myself through, after all those sleepless nights and terrible days of longing and sorrow, I was now waiting for her as one waits for a new, unfamiliar happiness. I held her hand and thought: Is this it? Is this Khanele? Had I not loved and longed for somebody else, a pious, shy girl afraid to look a man in the eye? She freed her hand from mine.

"You were surprised to see me yesterday, weren't you? Of course you were. You think I can't put two and two together? You think I don't know that Mother goes out to the theater with my uncle? She doesn't let me speak a word to anyone, I ask her why not? Is it some sort of sin? What do you think? You of all people should be able to teach me something—you Litvaks are natural born teachers after all—tell me, is it a sin?"

I was busy with my own thoughts and was only half listening to her.

"No, no," I smiled. I sensed a hidden message in her words. She had something to say and was trying to lead the conversation toward it. What was she trying to tell me? I took her hand and pressed it to my lips. She did not attempt to stop me. But I soon let go of her. I was kissing the wrong girl. A beautiful girl, true, but a stranger nonetheless! Just some girl I didn't know. I felt, then and there, that I had lost something very dear and important, something I might never get back. It was a pity, and it pained me. She broke the heavy silence: "I beg you, please, you won't say anything to my parents will you?"

Her voice wavered. She was suddenly silent, awaiting my response. I couldn't hold myself back any longer:

"That's it, is it?" I said angrily. "That's why you called me here today?"

But she didn't understand the tone of my reproach. She imagined that I wanted to take advantage of the situation, and so she offered me three rubles for my silence.

"Please, don't say anything," she said. I started to feel nauseated.

"Keep your three rubles!" I said sternly. "I won't tell anyone!"
Then I changed my tone and started speaking more softly.

"You know what, Khanele? Come, let's go for a little walk . . ."

A new feeling was growing within me, my eyes shining with sly
eagerness. We walked a while in silence. Coming to a quiet, narrow
side street, I stopped and made as if to embrace her, but she stood
stock still, gave me a stern look, and wagged a finger at me:

"Hey, Litvak!—No!" she said angrily. She knew how to give orders.
I stopped and didn't dare move another inch.

"Good night!" I just about managed to say and went on my way
with hurried steps. I was disgusted by my own crudeness, my love,
the three rubles, the world . . . I wanted to hide away from myself.

"Hey, Litvak! You'll take the three rubles!" she shouted after me,
and those were the last words I heard from my beloved.

1903

Neighbors

"A packet of Kabinet cigarettes."

Khayim-Borekh—a squat, stocky Polish Jew with a short, round, black beard who had just arrived from the provinces and now found himself selling cigarettes on the streets—almost slipped off the stick he'd been leaning on, and before he knew it, began automatically rummaging through his stock of cigarette packets.

The cold, frosty night was nearing midnight. A cloud of vapor hung in the air, exhaled by a Jew in modern dress who had stopped to buy cigarettes. He wore his coat with the collar up, and his out-stretched hand trembled in the cold.

"Kabinets!" he repeated impatiently. Receiving his cigarettes, he turned and hurried away. The sound of his footsteps lingered in the air.

Khayim-Borekh adjusted his makeshift perch: a stick atop which he had affixed a short plank of wood to sit on. Putting his hands in his sleeves to keep them warm, he sat back down with the expression of one who had been momentarily distracted from a more urgent matter.

The street was brightly lit. People were passing by less frequently now, and when they did, they walked briskly. They were visibly tired and frozen to the bone. The coachmen dozed in their carriages with drooping heads or chatted in fragmented, unfinished sentences. The big city seemed to sleep, and only the electric lamps in front of the restaurants still shone joyful and bright, looking down their noses at the rows of unlit city lanterns.

"Ten thousand," Khayim-Borekh started to think again. "Half of that is five thousand . . ." He pictured a packet of freshly pressed, red banknotes, crisp to the touch. He imagined himself back home in Grokhovtse—the packet of banknotes had become several packets that were arranged in orderly piles on the table. Then came Khaye-Leye and the children.

"Well? What do you say now, eh? I'm a nobody, am I?"

That last question, addressed to Khaye-Leye, to whom he felt somehow indebted, resounded so clearly in his mind that he mouthed it with his lips, and a tender smile appeared on his face.

"It's cold," he said to himself, standing up again. He removed the tray from around his neck and stamped his feet on the pavement. He looked around pensively.

He tried to position himself in such a way as to avoid the wind that blew with such hatred, chasing the frozen snow over the pavement.

"There now," he reassured himself, settling back down on his perch. His thoughts returned to his home and family, which were now transformed: the house had grown much larger, with a great big clock hanging on the wall. Everything was warm and bright. Khaye-Leye was dressed like a duchess. The children were clean and wore new clothes. Khayim-Borekh entered arm in arm with his neighbor, the Litvak, and said to his wife: "Here he is! Like I told you, a Litvak, but a decent person, a fine fellow. You thought he was going to swindle me with that ticket? Well, you're a fool, you daft woman. I told you right away. You'll have a glass of tea won't you, Mr. . . . Litvak?"

He realized that he didn't know the name of the Litvak he shared a room with in the basement apartment, this man who had convinced him to go halves on a lottery ticket, and that made him nervous. Stories that he had heard back home about Litvaks raced through his mind; he searched his pocket for the ticket and, finding it, felt calmer.

Earlier that day he had gone into a café with the express purpose of showing the ticket to some people, and they all reassured him that it was genuine, that the winning ticket would be drawn in five days, and that he would have a chance of winning ten thousand rubles.

Nestled close to his bent and frozen body, his head worked fast and vigorously, calculating his share of the prospective winnings, and he smiled.

Just then the electric lights went out; the last customers had left the restaurants. There were two girls skipping and smiling on the other side of the street, and Khayim-Borekh sank once more into melancholy and homesickness. He worried about the six rubles he had spent on the lottery ticket—he needed that money to pay for his trip home for Passover. He became angry with the Litvak.

"Something must be going on," he mused on the way home. "It can't just be how it seems." The thought that he had let himself be so horribly cheated, and that he would not be able to go home for Passover because of it, moved him to tears.

"Dear Khaye-Leye," he began, mentally dictating his wife a letter, "it's not my fault, I give you my word, I was tricked by a Litvak. You have no idea what those Litvaks are capable of—they could convince a stone! I swear it's not my fault. Forgive me, Khaye-Leye, and give my love to the children."

The corridor linking a whole row of basement apartments was dark. Khayim-Borekh found his way to the door by touch and fumbled with the handle. The cigarette tray clattered against the door, the sound echoing all throughout the corridor.

The Litvak opened the door for him. He was bare-headed and fully dressed, and had not slept.

"Why sho late?" the Litvak lisped.

Khayim-Borekh threw down his tray and sat on the chair; the cold and the exhaustion had caught up with him, and his feet were aching. He peeled off his boots, grumbling angrily.

"Why don't you answer me?" asked the Litvak, sitting down on his bed.

Khayim-Borekh felt like swearing at him, reminding him he was a Litvak, and that like all Litvaks he was a cunning heretic with no shred of Jewishness in him at all. Instead he said nothing. The lisp in the Litvak's pronunciation annoyed him, and it seemed as if in the *shhh* of that lisp lay hidden the whole essence of his deception. What bothered him most was that he could not tell the Litvak that he knew he'd been swindled.

"Why sho late, why sho late?" Khayim-Borekh said, imitating the Litvak as he took off his other boot.

"Come on though," the Litvak said, "five thousand big ones! Aha! Whad'ya say to that? Five thousand rubles! You understand what I'm saying?"

Khayim-Borekh's mind once again buzzed with thoughts of that five thousand, and he smiled while silently cursing the Litvak in his head.

An iron will you have: you could deceive a stone!

"Do you understand me or not?" continued the Litvak, standing up. "Do you still have the ticket? Let me have a look. You're such a backward *Itshe-Mayer*! So you're afraid, are you?"

"You swine of a Litvak!" said Khayim-Borekh with a smile. "My name's not Itshe-Mayer. You're swindling me and mocking me at the same time."

"God strike me down, who am I mocking? I'm telling you everything will be fine; you don't understand plain words? Ten thousand crisp ruble notes, I'm telling you. Ahaha!" He rubbed his hands together.

Khayim-Borekh smiled, looked at the Litvak's pale face, at his twinkling eyes, and beginning to feel some degree of trust, he asked, "You haven't swindled me then? Tell me the truth!"

"You're such a blithering idiot! I've paid six rubles from my own pocket and given you the ticket. What more could you want? What kind of people are you down here in Warsaw—halfwits, fanatical halfwits!"

Khayim-Borekh's heart sank and he lay down on the bed. He remained there for a long time, unable to fall asleep. The Litvak put out the lights and lay down on his own bed.

"What was it you said before, about fanatics?" Khayim-Borekh asked. He felt uneasy whenever the Litvak used a word he didn't understand.

"'Fanatics,' I said, you understand?"

"But what are *fanatics* exactly?"

"They're, you know, wild people like they have in America, who go around buck-naked . . ."

"Aha!" said Khayim-Borekh with a sigh.

He began reciting the nighttime blessing and dozed off. He soon started to snore; the Litvak became angry and grumbled.

"Fanatic! Complete fanatic! A nose like a shofar!"

Five days later, when the winning ticket was to be drawn, Khayim-Borekh woke up earlier than usual and, not feeling his customary morning fatigue, leapt out of bed and started to dress. Like anyone anticipating a life-changing event, he was nervous and on edge. It was just after dawn and darkness still covered the basement, which only had one small, high window. The Litvak called out from his bed, "God damn it, I didn't sleep a wink! It's day already?"

Not receiving an answer, he continued, "Today's the draw, you know. They'll send a telegram if we win. It'll come, mark my words. What will you do with the money? Admit it, you'll go straight to the Rebbe with an offering! Well, this is what I'd give him—bam!" and he stuck out his hand in the air, making an obscene gesture.

This blasphemy terrified Khayim-Borekh: he thought of atheism as a terrible affliction, like a contagious disease one must always be wary of, but he knew that it was better to say nothing. He gave the Litvak an evil look, washed his hands, and started putting on his tallis and tefillin.

The Litvak climbed out of bed, too, his disheveled hair covering his face. He hadn't slept well. He yawned and plodded toward the sink to wash.

A lamp still burned in the next room, and the cobbler who lived there was banging his hammer while whistling a song.

"Khane!" he called, interrupting his song to wake his wife. "Khane, get up and light the fire." Soon Khane roused herself from bed, a young woman, tall and pale, who reminded Khayim-Borekh of Khaye-Leye as she stood by the oven lighting the fire.

"Good morning to you, Granny!" said the Litvak boldly, looking up from the novel he had been glancing through while waiting for the tea. It was still quite dark in the room and he had trouble reading.

"Good morning, good morning, what are you two doing up so early?" asked Khane, rubbing a match that she couldn't light.

"Leave that," said the Litvak, going over to light the fire.

"A devil," thought Khayim-Borekh, putting down his tallis and tefillin and looking at the Litvak. He was jealous of his brazenness in calling Khane "Granny." It made him feel so weak, so helpless and timid. He could not understand why such a pious woman as Khane was so friendly toward him, when she knew he was an apostate who didn't pray, whereas he, Khayim-Borekh, was a pious Jew.

"An evil spirit," he thought, reminding himself what lay in store for the Litvak in the next world. He felt happier and cleverer than him, and he turned his attention back to the safety of his familiar prayer book with earnest pride.

Somehow they managed to avoid mentioning the ticket during breakfast, almost as if by agreement, and they went out into the street.

The day went by as usual—perhaps even faster than usual. By five o'clock Khayim-Borekh could no longer stand still on the street. He convinced himself that he needed to change his socks and went home. Looking around the room, he waited for someone to come and give him the news, but he soon grew restless. The door opened and the Litvak entered.

"What are you doing here, Reb Khayim-Borekh?" he asked cheerfully.

"I came, you know . . . eh . . . to change my socks."

For the moment neither of them mentioned the ticket. The draw lasted more than twenty days. Passover was fast approaching. With each new day, Khayim-Borekh's faith in the win shrank, and his hatred toward the Litvak grew.

"What a con artist! What a sinner!" he would curse him in his mind. But he held his tongue. The Litvak also appeared pensive and sad. They both endeavored to be the last to arrive home in the evening, so as to perhaps be greeted with a *mazel tov*. Once home, they avoided all mention of the ticket.

Khayim-Borekh's face had grown paler, and he walked with a

stoop. He wrote home that he would not be able to come for Passover. He wanted to pour out his heart to Khaye-Leye about the Litvak, that he had duped him, but for some reason he found it hard to write about it, and so his hatred toward the Litvak stayed in his heart and ate him up inside.

On the last day of the draw, Khayim-Borekh came home early and found the Litvak already spread out on his bed. He threw himself at him, cursing:

"Litvak! Swine! I should have known! You wanted to convince me that I could win! You swindled me out of six rubles for your sinful pocket! Give it here, I tell you! I don't even have the money to go home for Passover, you hear me!"

"Ah, what are you screaming for, Reb Khayim-Borekh?" he replied calmly. "What's the use of screaming? Sit down and we'll have a talk."

"Give me back my six rubles!" But Khayim-Borekh's voice lacked the conviction necessary to frighten the Litvak. Deep down he knew that the Litvak, too, had gambled away six rubles, and he blamed him only for being a free spirit, without a wife or children, heedlessly frittering away other people's money along with his own.

"Libertine!" he shouted. "What do you care, you apostate, that I won't be at home for Passover? You wasted money! What harm does it do you? Do you have a wife and children? Like hell you do!"

Not interrupting him, the Litvak simply said, "Don't be angry, Reb Khayim-Borekh."

Khayim-Borekh finally grew quiet and lay down, but he did not sleep at all that night.

The next day he loitered like a shadow. The yearning gnawed away inside him. He wanted to be with his wife and children, whom he had not seen in several months. Standing on the street with his cigarettes, he hung his head many times, wiping his damp eyes.

Passover came. Khayim-Borekh ate in a cheap restaurant full of young people, poor, clean-shaven heretics, some of them even without hats. He was sad and lonely. He feared that he might start crying in the middle of the Haggadah. Somehow the whole Seder went by without incident, lasting about an hour in all. Heartache kept him from eating, and he dragged himself home with a silent pain. He felt like he needed to pour out his bitter heart to someone, and he was ready to throw his curses on the Litvak. A barrage of oaths were already lined up in his mind, every last bit of invective he could muster.

But upon entering the room he was struck with a surprise. Lying in bed, the Litvak's eyes were wet, his face covered in tears. In shame he hid his face beneath the pillow.

"What's the matter?" Khayim-Borekh asked softly.

"Ah, it's nothing," replied the Litvak, trying to compose himself. He continued, "It's just . . . I'm homesick, I miss my wife and children, you understand? It's nothing."

"You have a wife and children?" Khayim-Borekh asked in shock.

The Litvak was clearly offended, and Khayim-Borekh could see that he too felt like shouting at someone, showering someone in curses.

"What did you think, Itshe-Mayer?"

"Don't be angry, please don't be angry," Khayim-Borekh pleaded.

They stopped speaking and listened to the various melodies that welled up from the other cellar rooms. In the next room over they had reached the verse "pour out thy wrath upon the nations," which the cobbler recited so sweetly that both Khayim-Borekh and the Litvak almost wept aloud. The candle started to flicker and went out, leaving only a blue light coming in through the window. The Litvak lay on the bed, wanting to sigh, to weep over his loneliness. In that moment Khayim-Borekh almost forgot his own situation, instead considering the plight of the Litvak, of poor Mrs. Litvak and the little Litvaklings who found themselves in some lost corner of Lithuania, and he felt great pity for them.

His composure regained, the Litvak called to Khayim-Borekh in a voice entirely free of his previous anguish.

"The lunar light is so beautiful tonight!" But remembering that Khayim-Borekh was a "fanatic" who probably wouldn't understand the word *lunar*, and sensing his discomfort, he added, "Look at the moon spinning around and around."

"Yes, of course," mumbled Khayim-Borekh from his bed.

"That's how it is," said the Litvak, pacing around the room.

"When there's no money it's bitter, I tell you, whether you're religious or not, it's all the same, I tell you. You think I was never religious? My grandfather was a rabbi; he also starved to death! It's all the same, I tell you . . ."

But Khayim-Borekh, realizing that the Litvak was on the verge of blasphemy, interrupted him and said: "Okay, okay, we'll talk tomorrow," and turned toward the wall.

1902

The Game of Love

For two hours now, he has been walking with her down one street after another. He feels happy, walking by her side.

Not happy exactly, but—almost happy. It seems as though any minute now, maybe in five minutes, something important and miraculous will happen: the last thin wall standing between one heart and the next will disappear. That glorious hour he has so long awaited, so long been hoping and yearning for, will finally come.

One more moment and everything will be different. Instead of petty, base thoughts, instead of foolish doubts and half measures, instead of these meager, impotent, broken feelings that possess neither function nor beauty—one single feeling will prevail, one beautiful, clear idea will spread out inside him, awakening life and courage in him like an invigorating light: the thought that this proud, young creature will become one with him.

Another minute, another five minutes, and there won't be a "he" who yearns for her and follows her like a shadow, or a "she" who moves one step closer and two steps back, pushing him away one minute and snuggling up to him the next, but one whole, two hearts in harmony: love!

The streets are quiet; the shops have already closed. The moonlight blends with the shine of the streetlamps in that particular luminosity reserved for summer nights in a big city. From above a rooftop the moon peeks out, bright and full, from behind a chimney, from around a street corner, hiding and revealing itself again as they walk. The night watchmen go past, their sticks tapping. From time to time a bell rings from a distant tower. There are few others out at this time of night. A drunkard staggers by, followed by a carriage whose wheels clatter on the hard cobblestones as it flies past. Behind a high church spire a pale cloud lurks silently, bathing in its own joy as though it has forgotten how to move. Here the road splits in two. The street on which they walk is long and wide, while the other, the one Manye lives on, is a narrow side street.

Bender came to a standstill and said: "I don't feel like going down the narrow street. Come on, Manye, let's walk a little more."

"No, Bender. It's late."

And yet she did not move an inch. She took a pocket watch out of her blouse to see how late it was. Bender grabbed the watch from her and refused to give it back. The small black watch seemed to him to be a part of Manye, and holding it in his hand gave him a certain pleasure, enlivening his smitten heart.

"A quarter to one," he said finally.

She stood pensively, then turned around and plucked the watch from his hand with an energetic flourish. Putting it away, she said: "All right then, let's walk some more. Everyone is asleep at home anyway. Where shall we go?"

"It's all the same."

And so they walk once more through the streets and squares; once again the moon hides and reveals itself; again they pass carriages and drunkards; and the tedious conversation about topics he has no interest in—theater, mutual acquaintances, and so on—continues interminably. Happiness is not coming. Bender once again starts to rebel against himself.

The old demons, which he has almost managed to smother, start to gnaw away inside his head again, this time stronger than before.

"Between us," he thinks, "there is no love, no harmony. There is nothing apart from a simple pact. She—an intelligent girl in search of a good life—wants to be with me, a young man who earns money, a good match for her . . . I am a fool, a child; I never understand what's going on around me."

He went silent as he became lost in such thoughts, and this silence, which she could still not grasp, irritated and insulted her. She was walking very close to him, trying to catch his eye, but he didn't say a word. He remained mute with a relentless stubbornness, and only by his downcast eyes and firmly shut lips could she see that something was on his mind. She was suddenly overcome by an impulse to find out what he was thinking, to find a way in.

"Why don't you talk to me?" she asked.

"Nothing's wrong, Manye," he replied, conscious of the fact that he was lying. "I just don't feel like talking. I only want to walk alongside you and be happy."

"What a terrible egotist you are!" she replied. "Always thinking about yourself, and never about others."

"That's true," Bender responded curtly. That answer, which she had often heard from him, wounded her. It seemed as though he was trying to hide his inner self. She answered angrily, "You always say that: 'That's true, Manye, that's true.' I don't need you to tell me I'm right. What I want to know is: why is it *not* true? You don't even think I'm capable of understanding you, do you?"

"You're right, Manye."

The conversation came to an end. Manye wanted to go home, and this time Bender did not attempt to stop her. He accompanied her to her door, and as they were saying goodbye he took her hand, pressed her fingers against his lips, and kissed them. Why he did that he had no idea, and he had the impression that the kiss was foolish and meaningless, like all of his deeds, like all of his thoughts and doubts.

Bender had once found himself in Manye's room, sitting right up beside her on the sofa. She had been in a good mood just a moment before, full of life and laughter, fidgeting and telling jokes. Her every movement seemed to call out: "I'm free as a bird, full of life, fresh and happy!"

But suddenly she became withdrawn and listless. Her hair was in disarray. It hung down over her shoulders, covered her ears, and obscured her eyes as it played trembling across her cheeks. Her small, dark face seemed to absorb her beauty. Her expression had grown rigid.

Her eyes seemed to have sunk behind a shadow of pain and longing.

She was wearing a light blouse. He stroked her hair, kissed her cheeks, her eyes, her forehead, and she spoke softly and imploringly: "What are you doing, Bender? Stop it, it's not right!"

But they were futile words that lacked any meaning, sounding to him like a faint echo from some wasteland. She belonged to him now; she was in his power. He turned her head toward him, making her shoulders tremble in his embrace and her slender, nimble arms hang limp and powerless; only her lips continued to beg: "Stop, Bender . . . for God's sake . . . what are you doing?"

Bender scolded her: "Be quiet! I don't want you to talk now!"

And he was shocked by his own voice. It was not the voice of someone in love but a cry of great pain. It was enough to bring him back to his senses, and to see his misery for what it was. He looked with compassion at the beautiful creature who sat shocked, will-less, and distressed next to him on the sofa.

"You don't love me, Manye! Tell me the truth . . ."

"I don't know, Bender; I respect you very, very much."

"And you're uncomfortable when I kiss you? You can't stand it?"

A tiny smile appeared on her lips. She started to feel free once more, proud and defiant. She went over to the small mirror on the table and began putting her hair in order.

"What nonsense you're talking today! You want to know everything. Brooding and brooding nonstop . . ."

"I let her out of my power, and now she starts biting and scratching again, like a cat," Bender thought.

"No, Manye," he said. "I don't like ambiguity, I can't stand it anymore. You're torturing me; you've stolen my spirit, I'm exasperated, agitated day and night. Tell me, please: do I disgust you? Can you stand my kisses?"

She paused for a moment, wrinkling her brow, and said: "One shouldn't be careless and let oneself be kissed by just anyone."

"And am I *just anyone*?"

She smiled again, satisfied, and answered: "I respect you very, very much."

And, as if to make amends, she sat back down beside him on the sofa.

He took her hand in his. She did not stir, waiting to see what would happen next.

"Tell me, Manye," he asked tenderly. "Can one kiss a person whom one respects?"

"And why are you asking that?"

"I want you to kiss me."

"Come now, Bender, please."

"No, I'm not giving up on you today," he said, holding back his agitation. "I must know, I must convince you, Manye . . ."

"You're acting very strange today, Bender! Stop, please . . ."

But he didn't let her say another word; he grabbed her head in both hands and pulled her face toward his.

"I'm not letting go of you until you answer me. I have to know, Manye. You have to answer: yes or no. Now! This minute!"

Her face had hardly touched his forehead when he felt a light flutter from her lips—a short, hasty kiss. Afterward, she went to sit on another chair, insulted and spent. Her gaze was filled with raw anger and mute pain. He stood up, kissed her on the forehead, and left the room, angry, agitated, his mood rattled.

Manye, Bender, and a few acquaintances had gathered in Bender's room one evening, talking and joking noisily. Manye, who had always played first fiddle in their little company, was in an even more high-spirited mood than usual. Bender was repulsed by her laughter, her movements—her every action seemed directed against him, specifically to annoy him. He sat by the table, concentrating on his book, irritated and taciturn. She found his outer calm exasperating, so she turned to him constantly, now with a joke, now with a question. He responded curtly and did not move from the spot. Lately Manye had the feeling that Bender was trying to distance himself from her, and she was not prepared to stand idly by.

Impulsively, she decided it was time to leave, and she called out in her melodious voice: "So who's going to walk me home tonight? Quickly, now!"

First to answer was Meyerzon, the third member of their group. He was young, handsome, healthy, and very lazy. He lived off the money that he borrowed from acquaintances and so was quite affable, with a permanently apologetic expression on his face. Girls generally liked Meyerzon, except for Manye, who did not feel any great affinity for him, and if she was sometimes nice to him, it was only to aggravate Bender. She had no intention of letting him walk her home. "Lie back down on the sofa, Meyerzon," she said. "I'm sick of you already. Gentlemen, who else would like to accompany me?"

Bender sat still, not moving an inch. He was fully charged with hatred. Everything the group said annoyed him.

"Not a single honest word, not one word without a hidden meaning ever comes out of her mouth!" he thought.

Everything about her rang false, base, and unworthy. He hated her deeply now and an urge for revenge welled up inside him.

But then she came near him, touching his shoulder eagerly and announced: "Bender will walk me home."

The slight touch of her hand threw him entirely off balance. All of a sudden his hostility evaporated; her mere touch stirred his whole being. He hadn't felt that stirring for a long time now; he'd missed it, even though it tormented him. He wavered over whether to go or not, but after one gentle glance from her he stood up, put on his overcoat, and exited with her.

"How blinded I was, Manye," said Bender as they walked together down the street. "For several months now I've felt like I've been standing on the threshold of happiness. Each day I've hoped to become a new person: that everything inside me would become calm, that my torn and tattered soul would breathe freely, and that you would grant me the happiness that I've only heard about from others, that I have never—not for a single moment—experienced for myself. I had hoped to find in you something to make sense of this bewildering life—I'm so tired of all this life, I can hardly breathe.

How wrong I was! Instead of happiness you gave me nothing but pain and hate . . ."

Manye interrupted him: "With you, I always have to give and give. You stand there with open hands waiting for people to give you things. You're always complaining, and always have to be right. Why don't you take your happiness, if you want it so much? You need to grab happiness, chase after it, not stand there like a helpless child waiting for someone to hand it to you. Why should anyone give it to you? How have you earned it?"

Her sharp rebuke shocked him, and he answered with feigned calmness: "It looks like we both hate each other enough. Maybe we should finish this, Manye!"

"What do you mean?"

"Shall we break up as friends or as enemies?"

Manye looked him in the eyes and answered with a smile: "You're all talk, Bender; we won't break up, I don't want to."

"But I want to, Manye."

"You don't really want to, Bender, do you?"

"Believe me, Manye, I want to. I have no energy left."

As they approached her door, she said: "Well then, Bender, give me your hand if you want . . . Oh, what a cold hand you have!"

She held his hand in hers for a moment and leaned over, as though she wanted to bring her young, fresh body closer. He could not stand the excitement and embraced her, kissing her vigorously. She pulled away with contempt.

"What is the matter with you, Bender? That's not a nice way to behave!"

That night Bender could not sleep, her final words would not leave his mind. Tossing and turning, he asked himself again and again: why, why had that happened?

The next morning Bender bought tickets to an outdoor concert and wrote to Manye, saying that he would be finishing work late and would pick her up. He was running behind schedule and hurried to get there on time. When he arrived at her place, he saw Meyerzon sitting in her room.

"The same old story starting again," he thought.

"Are you coming to the concert too?" he asked Meyerzon.

"What a question! Have you any idea what they will be playing tonight! You know, Manye, I would go without food or drink just to hear music. There are only two good things in this world: lying on the sofa and listening to music; there is nothing else. Do you not think so?"

"Original," responded Manye. "And you, what do you think, Bender?"

"I don't think anything at all. Let's go."

They took the tram. Manye sat next to Meyerzon, on the opposite side of the carriage from Bender, constantly whispering in Meyerzon's ear. Suddenly she laughed aloud, ignoring Bender like he wasn't even there. He sat as if on glowing hot coals. He wanted to jump off the tram and run away, and he would have done so if he had not been ashamed in front of Meyerzon. At the entrance to the venue, Manye turned to him: "How many tickets did you buy, Bender?"

"Two."

"And what about Meyerzon? Did you forget about him? We have to buy another ticket."

Reluctantly Bender bought a third ticket, although he knew full well that she had only brought Meyerzon along to annoy him.

"How strange it works out," he thought bitterly. "She forces me to help with my own torture!"

As they entered the open garden the orchestra was already playing. Meyerson barely heard a few bars before he was enchanted: "How beautiful, how wonderful! No loftier thing, I tell you, in the whole world than music. Listen! Listen! Incredible!"

Bender grew even more agitated. Here they were, in the garden, and Manye was still sitting by Meyerson's side. It was all meant as a deliberate affront. He felt insulted, tormented. And the music moved him to tears, penetrating his embittered heart, caressing and consoling it. For a moment he forgot all about Manye and Meyerson and the whole world and only remembered his own unhappiness, his own solitude, and the fact that there was nobody or nothing in the world about which he could say: "I love that, that's what I choose, that belongs to me." Sometimes a terrible hatred welled up again in his heart toward the unmerciful, unjust Manye. He felt that he must take vengeance on her—fire a bullet into her breast, killing her on the spot. A moment later and his spirit was calm, all thoughts of death retreating to a quiet corner of his brain.

"Like a dog, I'll die like a dog!" His heart cried together with the orchestra, and his eyes were full of tears.

The first half of the concert came to an end. He opened his eyes and saw Manye and Meyerzon stand up and begin walking toward him. He rose to his feet and left, without saying goodbye.

The next morning Bender was wandering in the streets. He felt tired and numb. He had been awake the whole night, had not gone to work, just wandered for hours without aim. Suddenly he saw Manye in front of him, approaching with hurried steps.

"Where did you get to last night?" she asked, offering him her hand.

But he didn't give her his hand. He did not even look her in the eye. She turned pale and started slowly backing away from him. Bender watched her until she was out of sight, and then continued on his way.

1907

Roommates

I

It was already well past midnight and the two roommates, who shared a bed in a cramped, stuffy apartment on the fourth floor, were still not asleep. The moon was not visible through the open window, yet it shone down onto the rooftops, which reflected its light—by now weak and diffuse—into the room. The day's heat still lingered in the air, and with it the smell of scorched roof tiles. In the landlady's room next door, the baby had only just stopped crying. There was a constant racket of carriages outside. Faint at first, the sound of the approaching carriages would grow louder and heavier, and just as it started to die down the clattering would begin anew. The whole house shook with each passing carriage.

The bed was cramped, the blankets had long ago been pushed aside, and the roommates, Fayner and Gutman, tried their best not to get in each other's way, turning from one side to the other and back again, flipping over their pillows. Their arms were a problem: whenever they tried to adjust their pillows at the same time their hands touched, and they flinched as if from a hot stove. They were both sweating, and the presence of each other's bodies reminded them of their own fleshy, sweaty selves: that which was born unclean grows and, eventually going the way of all flesh, falls apart.

They lay in silence, thinking. Fayner's thoughts, much like his movements in life, were agile, making quick connections, while Gutman's lumbered along slowly and heavily, like a wagon in the sand.

Fayner sat up and folded over his pillow.

"It's so stuffy," he said.

Gutman did not respond. He looked at his friend's upper body, waiting for him to lie back down. Fayner once again felt an animosity building up inside him toward his quiet, placid roommate, who was a lot more lonely and lost than he was and who tended not to think or speak much. Fayner lay back down, wiping his face with both hands.

It suddenly grew darker—the moon must have gone behind a cloud. Fayner turned over a few more times and thought about Gutman; during the four weeks they'd been living together he had never once seen him manifest the slightest enthusiasm or desire for anything. When visitors came to indulge in heated philosophical debates, Gutman would not join in, and during those moments it seemed as if he were hiding something: as though he had something to say, yet held his tongue.

Outside, a clock tower began to toll. They listened and counted. The clock struck two, and they both thought about how it would soon be getting brighter; the birds would start their cries, and only then would the roommates be able to fall asleep.

It was hard to tell if the brightness was from the reflection of the moon bouncing off the rooftops or if the sun had started to rise.

Fayner turned to face Gutman, and in the darkness he could feel Gutman's calm, melancholic gaze. Whenever he felt that gaze, his animosity would subside and he would think that Gutman was his friend, lonely like him, perhaps even more so.

"Tell me, Gutman, are you thinking about something?"

Gutman was slow to respond, and Fayner imagined that thin smile, which always offended him deeply, playing on Gutman's lips. He was about to turn around again when Gutman said softly, "It's two o'clock."

"Yes, it's two o'clock. I can't sleep, can you?"

"No."

They were silent for a few minutes, then Fayner said, "Tell me, Gutman, what were you thinking about just now? It's so dreary."

"Me?" Gutman asked groggily.

"Try to recall, and tell me."

Gutman said nothing.

"Gutman, you're not saying anything?" There was agitation in Fayner's voice. He felt it himself and was ashamed.

"I was thinking . . . no, never mind."

"Tell me."

"I was walking along Dzika Street this evening, by the edge of the city," Gutman said. His flat, mechanical voice and the Russian words coming out of his mouth resembled each other, as if cast in the same mold, and in the darkness they reminded Fayner of a clock ticking. "Poor people live there. There was a boy leaning against the wall in front of a shop; he was crying. Then he looked up at the sky and fell silent. Suddenly he remembered himself and started crying again, even louder."

"And?" asked Fayner, as his friend went quiet.

"Nothing; I was just thinking."

Gutman turned to face the wall. Fayner lay facing the window. Looking out, he saw a green, glimmering star that had just emerged from behind a cloud. He didn't want to think about Gutman and so tried to picture the boy and the neighborhood, which was not far from the Jewish cemetery. Of course Gutman went for walks there. Fayner remembered how once, as they were both coming out of the cemetery, Gutman had remarked: "It's strange that there's a prison next to the cemetery . . ." Now those words took on new meaning. Fayner turned and looked at the back of Gutman's head until his eyes grew tired and closed.

Outside, a bird called out, and a few minutes later other birds joined in until it was impossible to discern one bird's song from the other. Everything seemed to cry: the night that was coming to an end, and the new day that was beginning.

Fayner's thoughts became increasingly sparse, lighter . . . until he fell asleep.

Gutman lay awake. He was staring at a point on the wall, which became ever clearer and more in focus: this was his method of trying to fall asleep.

The commotion of the birds had already died down. The courtyard gate was open now, and the caretaker was sweeping up; you could hear a broom scraping against the cobblestones.

The baby in the next room cried long and hard until its mother heard. Gutman turned around. Fayner lay there with firmly closed lips, his brow furrowed, his face pale and full of wrinkles, his breathing deep and heavy.

The stained shirt on his shoulders rose and fell; he looked quite weak and helpless. The first rays of light shone on the rooftops—soon the sunlight would come into the room.

Gutman turned around again and resumed staring at the point on the wall.

II

They were poor, forsaken, and alone, living apart from the rest of the world. Their friends too were poor, forsaken, and alone. Fayner worked at a print shop, where he earned a few rubles a month. Gutman was looking for a job, though it was difficult to imagine he would ever find anything. In the meantime he wandered through the wide, noisy streets with his head down. The crowds stepped around him as they hurried past, as though he were a telegraph pole. Sometimes he would stop and fervently read the signage on the streets, before walking on until exhaustion forced him home. Once there, he would lie down on the bed and think. In the evening, when the sky filled with clouds, he sat by the window and gazed out. All he could see were rooftops and chimneys all around. The clouds hung so low it seemed like they might descend at any moment.

Darkness fell. In the distance the high spire of a church had already disappeared into obscurity. His surroundings coalesced into one sad, dreadful impression that weighed him down in the pit of his stomach. He sat silently, leaning on the window and squinting out into the darkness, which crept in from all sides. A small star flickered and then was lost. His eyes were tired; he stretched, rubbed his hands together, and said:

"That's it, yes. Yes."

Fayner had no idea what motivated his roommate or how he lived, and not knowing made him uneasy, stirring his mind and rousing his conscience.

One evening when it was pouring outside, Fayner came home expecting to find his roommate sitting by the window as usual, but Gutman was instead at the table. In front of him was a photograph. Hearing the door open, he turned around. They greeted each other, and then Gutman went back to looking at the picture with a rapt attention that Fayner had not known him capable of.

Fayner paced up and down, stealing a glance at the picture each time he passed it. It was a photo of a woman, a girl. Her face was pretty enough, her features symmetrical and harmonious, but they lacked a specific expression. He couldn't get a good look at her eyes from this distance, but they seemed calm and assured. The only thing that stood out was how her hair was combed: upwards into the air so that her whole high, charming forehead could be seen.

"Look, Fayner," Gutman said a while later, handing him the photograph very carefully, as though afraid Fayner would grab it from him.

"A pretty girl, indeed."

"A girl," Gutman repeated. "Do you see? Take a good look."

"I see a pretty girl, but there's no expression on her face."

Gutman smiled his thin smile and looked Fayner straight in the eyes with irony.

"You don't understand," he said with confident pride. "Have you ever seen a gaze like hers? Now that's a gaze . . ."

Seeing that his friend was so earnest and engrossed, Fayer had no desire to argue. Deep down he was happy to see him so enchanted, and being foolish for once to boot. But when he looked a little closer at the picture, those eyes acquired more expression, grew livelier, and the lips now seemed on the verge of saying something reassuring, something kind and lively.

"A relative of yours?" he asked. "I haven't seen you with this photograph before."

Gutman again measured him with a glance, smiled, and said

nothing. He continued to stare at the picture, and when the room started getting dark, he went over to the window, positioning the photograph so as to catch the light.

Putting it securely away in his breast pocket, he said: "There really is something special there. Oh yes. . . you wouldn't understand."

Gutman lit a candle and stuck it into one of several pieces of tallow that lay on the table.

Fayner lay on the bed watching his friend, who was now pacing distractedly around the room with slow, heavy steps. There was something off about him today. Fayner had never seen his face like this: so gentle, so lonely, and so open. "He's in love," he thought, and he began to look at Gutman differently: with the tender, kindly emotion that he would feel upon seeing two young lovers or small children.

"Sit down, Gutman," he said, pointing to the chair.

"What for?"

"Sit down, we'll talk."

Gutman sat down. "What is it?" he asked, fidgeting as though to stand back up.

"Sit," Fayner said, stopping him. "Show it to me."

"No need," Gutman answered haughtily. "You don't see anything there anyway."

"Well, I was wrong. I didn't look properly."

Gutman handed him the photograph, and Fayner, wanting to show that he was genuinely interested, sat down and bent toward the light to have a long look.

"Yes, yes!" he said, attempting to replicate his friend's tone.

"Yes, yes, you see?" Gutman said with delight. He looked at the card one last time before putting it away and falling silent.

Fayner brought over the kettle and served tea and bread. Somehow the room seemed more spacious, and in their cheer both friends decided to go to the theater the next day once Fayner had gotten his monthly three rubles.

When they had finished eating, Fayner stood up and said to Gutman with a laugh, "You're putting on weight."

"Me?"

"Yes, you," Fayner smiled. "You're so fat I'm sure I could never lift you. Want me to try? Get up, then!" he commanded.

Gutman stood up, sniggering idiotically.

Fayner wrapped his arms around him and lifted him up, quickly releasing him as he tired. The candle on the table fell over, rattling the glasses, and the room was plunged into darkness. Gutman wanted to relight the candle, but Fayner held him back, feeling strangely intoxicated.

"There's no need!" he said. "Leave it as it is. Well, now, it's your turn to pick me up."

"What for?" Gutman asked.

"Go on, my friend—pick me up!"

Gutman took hold of Fayner and lifted him up high. Then he deliberately set him back down.

Outside, the moon emerged from behind the rooftops; its light shone into the room and the two roommates felt suddenly self-conscious.

III

It was a hot summer. For days on end there wasn't a cloud to be seen. The sky appeared dusty, without a trace of color or character. In the evenings the streets teemed with tired, sweaty people rushing to and fro. Looking at their faces—which seemed to beg for respite from their constant suffering, tiredness, and bitterness—it was odd to think that those overworked people were the ones making all the racket. There wasn't a fresh face or free, lively movement to be seen. Trudging through the streets, sweaty and exhausted, Fayner felt driven to rush with the rest of the masses. He thought about his life up to that point, about everything he had ever done and said, and it made him feel like a spinning top that had been set spinning, spinning without volition. He was afraid to think about the future: whenever he did so he grew melancholic, and so he tried to suppress those thoughts. But once night had fallen and he had dragged himself home to his room, such thoughts became hard to stifle. He stood at the door for a few minutes, holding the handle, waiting. Once he lay down in bed, the heavy thoughts would burst into his mind from every direction, like pressurized water.

"An iron bed that's falling apart," he thought, "and four claustrophobic walls: that's what my life is. That's all it is!"

He barely spoke to Gutman. When they were together it felt as if there were a third person with them: a fresh, happy, lively creature. The only thing Fayner wanted to talk about was her, yet he did not dare begin. He reproached himself for being jealous of his friend, for being mean and bitter, for begrudging happy people their happiness. Gutman did not speak very much either. He kept mumbling something about needing to get a certain document in order to leave Warsaw. His passport was out of date and his trousers were ripped. But despite everything he remained calm and satisfied, as only a person in love can.

"You're happy," Fayner announced to his friend one morning. "You've got it easy. You don't need to go to the print shop every day, or worry about the proofs and galleys; you just hope and love."

He suddenly stopped, catching himself saying what he hadn't intended to say.

"My head hurts," he said, angry with himself for lying.

Gutman was still in bed, his hair full of feathers. One half of his face was bathed in sunlight, but he didn't seem to notice. He bit his bottom lip; there was something on his mind.

"Still no letter," he answered apropos of nothing.

"You really do want to leave Warsaw, then? Don't you like it here?"

"No, it's an interesting place, but everything is strange."

"I'm not sure what you mean. You don't like the people?"

Gutman looked at his friend askance, thought for a moment, and said, "I'm sure the letter will come today." He stood up and started to dress. Fayner went out to get rolls and tea. When he returned he was accompanied by a pale-faced young man with a small, black beard that looked as though it were glued on. As they came in, they met Gutman sitting at the table. He was holding the card and looking at it. Fayner's acquaintance did not want to eat. He paced back and forth across the room, holding his cane and gesticulating with it as he spoke, his eyes fixed on the floor.

"It's a scandal! Those French socialists, invited into a bourgeois ministry and waltzing right in! It's a scandal, I tell you! A scandal!"

Suddenly he approached Gutman, and, spying the card in his hand, he slapped him on the back. "Well, well, well, let's have a look then. What? Ptui!"

He spat on the floor.

Gutman looked at the saliva stain, then wordlessly caught Fayner's eye.

The mood had turned sour. The acquaintance soon took his leave with a brusque, "At any rate, I have no time to waste on you two."

Gutman seemed angry that Fayner had told someone about his love affair. Fayner felt guilty and foolish.

He read in Gutman's expression: *you're a loathsome human being, a foolish blabbermouth!* He couldn't justify himself. He left his tea unfinished and, halfway down the stairs, felt as if he had been driven from his own home, wondering why he wanted anything to do with Gutman.

"What does he want from me? I don't understand. I don't understand anything!" he repeated to himself, his gaze darting around at the high buildings and the people in the streets. Life had never made much sense to him; everything he had ever said or done had lacked any will of his own, like a reflex.

He dashed across the street, not knowing where he was going; he crashed into several people, and each time they stopped and looked at him questioningly as if to say, "Are you mad?"

Out of nowhere, as though gripped by an invisible force, he stood still and said to himself: "Let me think."

The bell on the high church tower began to ring. A woman knelt down in prayer. There was a policeman watching him from the corner of the next street.

Fayner wanted to think clearly for once, wanted to know where one thought ended and the next began, but as always, after a few seconds on the street he couldn't remember what it was he needed to think about, and so he continued on his way with slow steps.

It was ten o'clock, but Fayner did not feel like going to work. He was in no state to read the proofs that awaited him there. He drifted down another couple of streets and remembered that he had met an old acquaintance there the previous day. The acquaintance, who once upon a time had shared all of Fayner's passions and interests, had gotten married two years ago and was now in the rental business, living in a summer house not far from Warsaw. Whenever they bumped into each other his acquaintance would smile, somehow managing to drag Fayner down the street with him for quite a ways, and each time Fayner was piqued by that smile, and by his own weakness in allowing himself to be drawn along. The last time they had met, the acquaintance had invited him out to his summer house for a visit sometime, if ever he was free.

"Come in the morning," he'd said, "and you can be back home by evening."

"And really," thought Fayner, "I haven't been out of the city in such a long time."

He set off in a rush toward the train station. He had the feeling that someone was chasing him, and that it was Gutman.

"What does he want from me?"

Fayner was struck with such self-pity that he felt like crying.

The fields, which stretched far and wide, were bright and full of vegetation. Fayner stuck his head out the window, and his eyes rejoiced, taking it all in. On the horizon he could see a forest that resembled a black strip. Above the strip, whole hordes of clouds of every size were gathering, following behind Fayner's train in grim silence. The foreground rushed by while in the distance the horizon remained calm and still. The constant whistling of the locomotive disturbed him. The train made many stops, and by the time he arrived at the last station he did not feel like getting off; he would have liked to stay there with his head stuck out the window.

Exiting the carriage, he once again felt uneasy; he would have to ask around to find out where his friend lived, then pay him a visit, meet his wife, talk, and maybe eat there. The mere thought of it exhausted him. The train had already gone, and he was left standing at the station, lost in his thoughts. The few passengers who had gotten off at the station kissed those waiting for them on the platform. A young boy held an older man's hand, clearly his father's, and kissed it. The father was in a hurry and walked quickly, carrying a suitcase in the other hand. The child followed, unwilling to let go of his hand. Soon everyone had gone, as though hiding like the birds somewhere behind the trees. Fayner saw no one else around, apart from the guard who stood with a trumpet in his hand and a pensive expression on his face as he watched the line.

He strolled down a road between two rows of villas. There were people on either side. Somewhere, someone opened a curtain, and Fayner quickened his pace, feeling that he was being followed on both sides by strange looks: *Who is that? What's he doing there? Where does he live?* He had no answer for any of these questions. But once he had passed the villas unscathed, he felt better and looked up. He emerged onto a square surrounded by trees; clearly it was an abandoned place where nobody went. The ground was sandy, only sparsely topped with grass. There were several stunted trees struggling to draw moisture from the sand. They seemed sad and lonely. From inside the forest came the sound of swaying branches and the cawing of crows. It was quiet there. Fayner felt free from human scrutiny, and from himself. The sun burned, and the sky was pure, blue, and deep. Fayner had not seen a sky like that in a long, long time. He walked around for a while, and not a single thought stirred in his mind. His head began to feel heavy, his temples pounding: one, two, three . . . The heat continued to torment him, and it became harder and harder to drag his feet.

Lying on the forest floor, he fell asleep. When he opened his eyes, the sky was visible through the branches directly above him. A cloud passed slowly and lazily. Movement could be heard from afar in the trees, and several birds were chirping.

A feeling of pure laziness filled him. He felt the earth beneath his chest and the beating of his heart on top of it, and he did not want to move a single muscle. What had happened earlier that day all seemed like a dream, and he wanted to continue dreaming. But he heard nearby the sound of human voices, laughter, and running, and he bolted upright. Not far from him, through the trees, ran a group of young girls and schoolboys in a whirl of gaiety. He hurried out of the forest, still not able to recall clearly when and how he had come to be there. He felt as if someone had nudged him while he slept in order to ask him something, but he had been too tired to open his eyes.

The sun was already low. He still had about two hours before his train, so he walked slowly down toward the track and into the shed that served as a station. He sat down on a bench, crossed his arms, and looked off into the distance.

Next to him stood the same guard from before, in the same position. Standing still as a signpost, he watched the line. Fayner could picture more clearly now how he had spent the day, fleeing his room for this unfamiliar place where he did not belong and could only get in people's way. His heart once again felt heavy. He looked toward the trees, behind which many villas lay hidden, and he thought about how those who are happy and satisfied hide themselves away, keeping their happiness secluded from unfriendly eyes. If someone were to permit him to enter into their room tucked away in the forest, he would bring in his unhappiness, spoiling everything with jealousy and hate. He thought about Gutman: even Gutman was happy, and he hides his happiness away—oh, how he hides it! Only he, Fayner, went around with his heart displayed like an open book for everyone to see, making a burden of himself for everybody.

"Oh, God!" he sighed.

A dark figure emerged from the trees: a slender woman dressed in black. As she came up to the platform she adjusted her hair, pushing it out of her face and over her brow. She walked slowly, her gait sure and graceful, and when Fayner met her eye she looked away. Her gaze struck him tenderly and lightly, but it lingered on his face with authority: she had looked at him because she wanted to look, and she looked for as long as she needed. She was very striking, and there was something about how she combed her hair over her brow, which she clearly wished to accentuate, that stuck in Fayner's mind, seeking an explanation.

More people arrived, mostly young boys and girls dressed in light, loose clothing. You could hear the rustle of summer dresses, pieces of gravel springing underfoot, faces that were either smiling, preparing to smile, or resting between smiles. Since he already had his ticket, Fayner wandered among them, occasionally brushing past a dress. He was happy to find himself surrounded by so many people, and to be free, entirely free, doing what the others were doing; he had a ticket just like them. But each time he passed the girl in black, he felt uneasy and couldn't shake the sense that something was about to happen, something very important.

The sun was only now starting to set. You could imagine that some giant hand was turning a wheel beneath the sky, slowly changing the decoration so as not to scare anyone. The lanterns lit up.

The girl rose and walked several paces along the platform. Fayner stopped in his tracks: he recognized her.

"It's her, it's her, her . . . it's Gutman's girl!"

A locomotive whistled in the distance. Someone shoved past him. The moon peered out from behind the forest. Toward the west everything was so silent and still that he felt like heading out in that direction, with all his negative thoughts.

IV

It was night by the time Fayner arrived in Warsaw. He was exhausted and his head ached. Everything in him felt unscrewed; nothing was in its right place. Thoughts of Gutman and his lover's mysterious appearance at the station had not left him the entire journey. He could picture her: beautiful, calm, wrapping her arms around Gutman, kissing him . . . and Gutman—self-satisfied, secure in his belief that he deserved it—smiling and slowly kissing her. Fayner rubbed his hands over his face several times, struggling to banish the image from his mind. But he was haunted by her eyes, and at times it seemed as though the border between Fayner and

Gutman had vanished: instead of Gutman embracing her, it could have been him.

He remembered an evening when he had been walking through the streets. He had been contemplating the idea of Gutman getting married—he would have a beautiful, clean house, and Fayner would be a welcome guest. Fayner could not fathom how that thought had once seemed so pleasant and now seemed so terrible.

He did not go straight home, as he dreaded finding Gutman there and didn't know how he was going to talk to him, so he wandered the streets. A pale moon trembled in the sky as if afraid. The city's bustle had not yet come to a standstill, and policemen watched him from every street corner.

He grew tired, wanting nothing more than to lie down; once again he felt chased from his own room.

It was already past two when he came home. He snuck through the front room like a thief and passed into the bedroom. Without lighting the lamp he got undressed and slipped into bed. He imagined that Gutman was awake and listening, only pretending to be asleep.

Fayner turned his back to him, closed his eyes, and fell asleep.

In his sleep he heard someone enter quietly, sit down on the chair, and begin banging slowly on the table with his fist: one, two, three, four ... after each bang the figure leaned back, as if waiting for a response. Fayner understood that this intruder was trying to wake him, so he tore himself from sleep.

"Who's there?" He shouted.

Gutman—who was still in bed next to him—stirred but did not speak. Trains whistled in the distance, conversing with each other. It was already morning.

"Gutman, was someone here?"

Gutman stirred again and did not answer.

Fayner bit his lip and looked at Gutman's tangle of messy hair, at his face, and as he once again imagined those two soft, fresh arms embracing Gutman's grubby body he felt a terrible hatred toward him, so full of his own happiness that he would not acknowledge the suffering of others.

"Loathsome human being," Fayner muttered, turning away.

When he woke again later in the morning, he checked to see if Gutman was still there. He recalled some incident during the night. Opening his eyes he saw that the room was empty. He remembered insulting Gutman, who must have gotten dressed at dawn and gone out.

"What's happening to me?" he mumbled, burying his head in the pillow. "What's happening to me?"

He needed to hurry to the printers. With relentless efficiency, he worked without pause. At three, he finished up and went out to search for Gutman. His roommate was in one of the wide streets, sitting on a bench with his head in his hand, staring at a bicycle.

"What are you doing here?" asked Fayner, feeling agitated. "I've been looking for you."

Gutman stood up and stared long at Fayner, unselfconsciously, just because he wanted to. Fayner once again remembered the gaze of the girl the previous evening.

"I was sitting here," he answered after a short pause, and sat back down on the bench. Fayner sat down beside him.

"Tell me," Fayner began, his voice uncertain, "are you angry with me? It's not my fault; you know my nerves are on edge."

"You talk like a child, Fayner." Gutman looked him right in the eyes, with irony. "I'm in your way. The letter isn't coming; I have to leave today."

"But you can't leave today; you don't have any money."

"Next week I'll have a little money. I'll sleep here under the bench. I have a passport; nothing will happen to me." He spoke firmly, trying to convince himself that he would do it.

Fayner attempted to smile. He was completely at a loss and didn't know what was happening. Gutman wanted to go away, but what about the girl? And what did Fayner want?

"You won't leave, Gutman. Please, it's not my fault, believe me ..."

Gutman interrupted him. "Where were you yesterday?"

"Oh yes, I forgot to tell you, I was invited to visit an old friend at his summer house out in V___. It's lovely out there, very nice. We should go sometime. What do you think?"

It seemed to Fayner that his words had agitated Gutman, who must have been uncomfortable with the idea of the two of them going out there together, where she lived.

"Let's go, then," said Gutman. "It's been a long time since I've seen a field, but I won't come in to see your friend."

They had seats opposite each other on the train. At first Fayner stood by the window, looking out, thinking that everything was like the day before, but not knowing where yesterday's joy had gone. Then he gave up the window to Gutman, who stared for a long time and said: "Just like back home, the same houses and the same farmers."

Fayner was growing impatient; the train was moving very slowly and the carriage was full of smoke. There were ill-tempered, nervous faces all around that reminded him of his own face.

Gutman was still standing by the window. "We're here," said Fayner, touching his roommate gently on the shoulder. "Come on, then."

They looked at each other for a moment in silence, their gazes full of uncertainty.

As they got off, Fayner could have sworn that Gutman already knew the place. Without a word he marched straight in the direction that the girl had come from the previous day.

"Where are you going?" Fayner asked. "There are only villas over there."

"That doesn't mean we can't walk there, does it?" Gutman asked, looking all around. "It's nice out here; you know I hate the big city."

Fayner did not answer. As they followed the train tracks Fayner kept looking back toward the station.

"Let's sit down," Gutman said, throwing himself onto the grass. He rested his head on his hands and looked up at the sky. Fayner sat down beside him.

"Do you know who I saw here yesterday?"

Gutman looked straight at him and turned away again. Clearly he wasn't interested in what Fayner had to say. He took the photograph out of his breast pocket and stared at it.

"Let me see for a minute," Fayner asked.

Gutman handed him the photograph and bit his top lip. Fayner looked at the picture; a pair of confident eyes stared back at him. Fayner's hands were unsteady. Gutman observed him carefully. Fayner once again felt shaken.

"I don't understand," he thought again. The photograph fell out of his hand; Gutman picked it up, wrapped it in paper, and put it back in his pocket.

"Come," said Fayner.

"What for?" Gutman asked calmly.

It was silent. The sun shone over the forest. Gutman was startled by a frog that jumped suddenly out of the grass nearby.

Fayner called out: "You know who I saw here yesterday? Have a guess!"

Gutman looked him sternly in the eye. "Who?"

"Her," he said, pointing toward Gutman's breast pocket.

Gutman sat down, shielding his eyes from the sun with his hand. He smiled scornfully. "You're lying; you don't even know her."

"Yes I do know her," said Fayner, beginning to lose his temper.

"Come on," Gutman said. "Don't lie. You don't know her."

"If you want, I can point her out to you today."

"You'll point her out to me?"

"Yes."

"Go on, then!" Gutman answered with resolve.

Fayner's heart was thumping when they got to the train station. He felt like he was steering someone toward a disaster. He spotted her from afar, sitting and looking in their direction. Gutman walked quickly, his steps faster than usual.

Fayner lowered his gaze as they walked past her.

"Did you see?" he asked.

"Where?"

"There!" He shoved him by the arm. They wandered up and down a few times, not saying a word. Fayner had no idea what was happening. He looked toward the west, remembering the big, bustling city that lay just beyond the forest. Relieved when the train finally approached, he went to buy tickets.

Fayner stood leaning by the window, almost afraid to look his friend in the eye. Gutman was silent. Night fell outside. Clouds covered the sky and a drop of rain hit Fayner in the face. He sensed movement behind him and noticed Gutman was throwing pieces of torn card out the window. One piece landed on Fayner's shoulder; he looked at it and recognized the familiar arm of the girl. A chill ran down his spine.

He turned around to see Gutman sitting, arms crossed, staring down at the floor.

"You tore up the photograph?" Fayner asked, curling his lips in a smile. "You're a strange one. Why did you tear it up?"

Gutman answered in a low voice: "What? A girl like any other, but what good is she to me?"

"But where did you get the photograph? I thought . . ." Fayner could not finish; something caught in his throat.

Gutman smiled, moved his lips strangely, and said: "I was wrong."

The clouds grew thicker overhead. Fayner leaned his head out into the darkness, wanting to lose himself in his thoughts. His mind was as silent as a graveyard. But suddenly he remembered the boy Gutman had told him about: the boy who cried and looked at the sky. He could picture it so clearly now, the boy in a torn kaftan, leaning against the wall, and he lost himself in thought.

V

It was dark in the cramped room, the night pressing in against the windows. Rain beat down on the rooftops, and the wind blew in through a half-broken pane. The two friends lay in silence, as far away from each other as possible. Gutman watched the window, picturing the heavy rain clouds that were now moving over the sky, without beginning or end. He recalled a particular rain shower from his youth, when he had stood in the schoolyard looking at the horizon, waiting to see when the last cloud would appear. Dark clouds such as those were passing overhead now, and he lay calmly, silently, indifferent, as if it had nothing to do with him. But in the darkness, an idea flashed, and his mind lit up. Gutman took comfort in his own thoughts: he could count on them and very rarely shared them with anyone. But this time he felt the urge to talk.

"Fayner, are you asleep?" he asked cautiously.

"No. Do you want something?" Fayner turned to face him.

"Listen, what would it be like if people didn't have eyes? Have you ever come across anything like that in your books?"

"I might have . . ." Fayner was troubled by his words.

"You might have? Well, just imagine if we couldn't see anything, if no one could see anyone. It would be dark. What would we do if we happened upon an unfamiliar hand in the darkness? Just imagine!"

"What?" Fayner asked, shocked.

"Imagine with what joy you'd hold that hand! What joy! Do you understand?"

"I'm afraid I don't understand at all. You know . . . I was jealous of you before . . . let's go to sleep."

1902

Letters

Yankev Bender, a tall man of about thirty, with a thin, pale, clean-shaven face, paced back and forth across his room, his brow furrowed, deep in thought.

On the table lay a letter he had just received from Rokhl, the very girl he had not let out of his sight for the last two years. He could think of nothing else. Whenever he walked past the table, his gaze fell upon the letter.

His mind was anything but clear, yet he glowed with satisfaction and triumph and felt uncharacteristically invigorated; he could have paced around the room for hours, giving himself over entirely to those light, anxious thoughts and emotions. They gave him a sense of relief, as though someone were calmly stroking his hair, whispering: "You are a serious, worthy, decent man, Bender."

All the while, the words that Rokhl had carelessly let fall in her letter echoed in his fantasy: "After everything that's happened, I have to admit that I didn't know you. Do you love me?" Each time those words came to mind a contented smile played on his lips, and he remembered what Rokhl had once said to him: his laugh was strange, even when he laughed his face retained its usual earnest and sad expression.

Back when she had said those words, he had taken them to heart and they had rankled him. Now, though, the idea evoked pleasure, even pride, like everything else that passed through his mind.

His musings were interrupted by the creaking of the door behind him. The maid, a young, pretty Christian girl, passed through the doorway and stopped, as if afraid to come any closer.

"Would sir like some tea?" she asked.

Bender nodded, smiled, and said, "I'll have some tea."

The maid looked particularly pretty at that moment; the green lamp lit up her face and chest, adding a certain charm to her simple beauty. As usual, she remained a while. Everything about Bender struck her as peculiar: his intolerable gaze, his curt answers, and his nervous, agitated movements, all of which offended her female pride.

She was used to young men that she had to push away as they chased after her, trying to kiss and grab her. Bender didn't say much to her and never tried to kiss her; he never even touched her. And yet whenever he took even one step toward her, she panicked and turned pale. She couldn't shake the feeling that he was going to pounce.

Bender, in good spirits, turned to her with a smile.

"Does Marysia have a fiancé?"

"A fiancé? Where would I get a fiancé? I don't need one."

"But . . ."

Bender felt suddenly uneasy and would have been happy if she left the room, but she just stood there by the door and said with a laugh: "I did have a fiancé. I was engaged for two years. If I had enough money, I'd be married by now."

"Good, good, you can bring in the tea then."

The maid left and returned with tea. She again idled by the door, looking at the back of Bender's head as he hunched over the table, lost in thought. He felt her burdensome nearness and went out of his way not to turn around.

Eventually she left. Bender got up and resumed pacing, composing a letter to Rokhl in his head.

"I have never told a lie and I never will," he thought with pride. "I will try to give you my heart, bare as it is; I want to be myself with you." He stared for a while at the paper in his hand and then started to write.

Dear Rokhl,

I have only just now received your letter, which so filled my heart with gratification and joy that I hasten to answer you, paying no heed to the gravity and the seriousness of the question you have presented. I want to speak for once from the heart, to explain things to you, my dear, and at the same time make my feelings clear to myself.

I have already told you that ever since I found a job and started leading a decent, regular life, I feel unsatisfied and miserable. My nerves are even more on edge now. One after another, my old acquaintances distance themselves from me as if I had committed a terrible sin. And to tell the truth, I do feel like I've sinned ... why? I don't know. Perhaps because I'm used to living in dirty, cramped rooms rather than eating my fill or sleeping well. I'm used to going hungry; in a word, I've made my peace with poverty. It's always hard in the beginning. I'll get used to it and then I'll live like everyone around me, come what may! You could call me "bourgeois," one of the crowd, but there's one thing I won't let them take away from me, one thing I know for sure: I've never lied. I've never even *wanted* to lie. And yet believe me, my dear, ever since my childhood I haven't managed to converse with someone without having the shameful feeling that I was hiding something from them, that I was giving myself airs, that I was not who I said I was. But with you, my dear, I've spent many hours without knowing that distasteful, guilty feeling. And even now as I write to you, my heart feels free and true.

You were surprised by my behavior the whole time you were here. I did not say a single clear word to you. Not once did I press your hand lovingly; that must surely have offended you. I realize that, but what could I have done? You have to understand that for all my searching and striving, and despite everything that has filled my life with meaning, so to speak, that after ten years of wandering I was left with nothing I would consider important. You, my dear, are the only thing I have left. I have thought about you a great deal. Could I pick a single word from the dictionary that would feel right to say to you? Could I lie to the only creature to whom I felt a connection? No! I could not do that; you are too dear to me. I did not want to feel as though I had sinned against you.

Do I love you? Yes, certainly.

I remember one evening in your room; you laughed and looked very beautiful. Your hair and your whole tender, young body seemed to laugh with you. The piercing fire that once burned in your black eyes, rebuffing me whenever I wanted to get closer to you, was gone. You were pure levity and joy. And I remember that each time you laughed, I felt as though a waterfall were crashing down upon my brain; I grew tired and lay down on the sofa. You came over and pulled me by the hand. I seem to recall you saying: "Look how he's stretched himself out!" And—that moment is vivid in my memory—it was like a powerful current was flowing through my whole body. I wanted to embrace you, to fall upon your neck and cry. But I couldn't do that in front of the others. And when you pulled away from me, my whole body shuddered, as if in a fever. A great lightness overcame me; my head was empty and I felt only that flowing current, forever frozen inside me . . . That night when I got home to my room, I no longer felt alone or isolated—I was happy. But the feeling was only temporary, and many, many times I wanted to say something to you but could not.

You no doubt remember last summer at Shavuos, when we went for a walk together just outside the city. We left our companions behind and walked ahead, just the two of us. Suddenly you ran up a little hillock. You were very pretty then, young and fresh and full of life. You stood there like a tree in full bloom.

I remember your face, your hair, and the last rays of sunlight playing on them, the way your eyes gazed with such softness and longing at a small house far in the distance, how they sparkled, bathed in light. I remember the look you gave me, and how you suddenly jumped down from the hillock with outstretched arms . . . right then I wanted to run and embrace you. But I was too late: the others had caught up with us. Something always held me back; that feeling always died in my heart before it had a chance to come out into the bright world.

When it was time for you to leave, I accompanied you to

the train station. The idea of doing something obsessed me—
but I held my tongue. I didn't know what to say. Shortly before
the train started to move, I knew that everything would stay
the same as always. I dreaded the moment when you would
disappear, leaving nothing but an empty space before my eyes.
I thought something must happen—I would cry, or laugh, or
scream . . . and I came home with an empty heart.

I don't know what's wrong with me; I'm starting to get dizzy. I hear people speak about love, hate, jealousy, and various
other things. Sometimes I think it's all just talk, that they are
not sincere, that there's really no such thing as love, or hate,
or jealousy, or anything like that. There are just thousands of
ephemeral emotions bearing no resemblance to each other.
There is only the individual, who changes from one minute to
the next. And when I think like that, I feel better. Those moments make me think I'm better than the others, a pride that
I have carried for many years. Then I say to myself: the reason
why I can't live is because I'm clever, because my eyes are open.
But this only happens rarely. Normally I think: "What if?" Who
knows . . . maybe my heart really is so corrupted, maybe only
my life is so fragmented. Maybe the fault lies in the ten years
I spent wandering without family or friends, without a home,
without a female companion?

I'm telling you all this so that you'll know the state of my
soul, so that you'll understand why I held my tongue and did
not utter those few words that could have bound you to me.
I said nothing because I wanted to be sure, because I did not
want to lie.

If I had previously loved at some point in my life, I could
have compared what I felt for you to past romances, and I would
have known. But I had never loved, never embraced, never kissed
a woman . . .

Bender suddenly stopped writing. His face contorted into a
strange scowl, his mind reeling as it did whenever he remembered

an ugly incident from three years ago in another city, with a different girl whom he had treated similarly to Rokhl. When they were alone once he embraced her without warning, and she pushed him away, screaming: "Scoundrel!"

A few seconds passed before Bender's head cleared and he scribbled the word three times on a scrap of paper: "scoundrel, scoundrel, scoundrel."

He paced around the room before continuing the letter.

There's one thing I know for sure. From childhood on, whenever I shake with laughter and feel my emotions surge, one thought always hides in the corner of my mind: "If you wanted to, Bender, you could be calm." That voice always speaks from deep inside me.

So, my love, I pointlessly burden you with my letter. Forgive me. I have to be what I am, at least for one living being, for you.

Do I desire you? Yes! How easy it is for me to answer such a question. Yes, yes, and yes! What's more, apart from you I have nothing. Living without you is impossible. I have no friends, no family, no trusted companion. My acquaintances distance themselves from me; there's nothing to connect us anymore. I'm lonely, full of revulsion and disgust.

It will be good here for you, my dear. I will love you—ah, how I'll love you! I can picture it now: we'll sit together at lunch. I'll stand up satisfied and agreeable and I'll kiss your forehead, your beautiful forehead. You don't know how deeply I can love; my heart has never been lacking.

The door opened and the maid came in to take his glass. Bender put away his pen. The maid's shoulder brushed against him, and he stared at her absent-mindedly in silence.

"Would sir like anything else?" she asked.

"Hmm," he smiled crookedly and stood up. The maid left the room.

Left alone, Bender looked at the letter, at the sheets of paper with writing on both sides, and yawned.

He was already sure that he would not send it, that his present bout of agitation was no different from all the others. His tendency to philosophize and ponder was a foolish, childish habit that had poisoned his life for as long as he could remember.

"What I've written here to Rokhl," he thought, "I could have said to any remotely good-looking girl. I could even have said it to the maid."

The sheets of paper lay scattered on the table. He was afraid to read them through from beginning to end. Once again he felt overcome by exhausting thoughts, and to distract himself he lay down on his bed and started humming a Russian song. His heart wandered longingly toward the subject of the song, a woman who boated across a river with her lover one fine evening. He was intoxicated by the idea of a full life of joy and desire, of health and strength, that the song promised. In his imagination he saw the boat with its sails unfurled in the wind, the stillness of the water, the evening air. He felt the strong, healthy body, a young ruddy face . . .

But suddenly, seemingly from nowhere, a sobering thought came into his mind.

"I don't know what's happening around me! I'm a fool," he cursed himself, pacing angrily across the room. "What do I even want? What is my desire? What am I philosophizing about? I want to live. I'm tired! She wants to marry me; why turn my nose up at it? Do I not have the right to take a wife? Who am I afraid of? Who? Why?

"Lies, lies, lies," he added angrily when he remembered the words of the letter: "I can't live. Lies, I can live, I can!"

The thought that, in reality, he was incapable of living like others, that his laugh was a sort of sigh, as Rokhl had once said, weighed down his heart. He bit his lower lip in rage, and in a frenzy he went back to the table and wrote Rokhl an entirely different letter:

My life, my soul!

I keep reading and rereading your letter and can't believe how happy I am. It's right here in front of me, written in your own hand, your small, pretty, white hand. Oh! How much I would love for you to see what's happening in my heart! *You,*

you are talking to *me*. I read each word, each letter, and I ask myself, am I really happy? Do you belong to me, Rokhl? I love you, how I love you! It was only due to so much love—my heart was filled up to the brim—that I could not speak. I couldn't. I didn't want to turn the holiness of my love into something mundane. We are happy, after all! I have just now received your letter, and I can't hold back my feelings. I kiss you and love you without end. My life and soul—I am yours, yours, yours! Imagine: after ten years of wandering without a spark of love, without even a spark of life, I've suddenly become happy, the happiest person in the world, because you belong to me, my dear love. I kiss you and press you to my heart. Tomorrow I'll write to you at length and discuss everything in detail. My happiness has made me drunk, I'm crying, shedding tears of happiness, yours . . ."

"Yes, I can," Bender thought as he finished reading the letter. With the feeling of a conqueror he leaned back in his chair and stared in front of him. The first letter lay there on the corner of the table, and it waved silently like the hunted, insulted truth, demanding that which belongs to it: the juices of life, blood and marrow.

"Well?" he asked himself, should he send the second letter?

He read it through again and pictured how Rokhl would read it, how surprised she would be to hear such words from him, her difficulty in reconciling the letter's tone with his usual behavior and manner of speaking.

He sat a while in silence, tired and weary, his head empty of thoughts.

"What will I do?" he asked himself again and suddenly had an idea: bringing over the little bottle of glue, he stuck both letters together and wrote with a red pencil on both sides: "Choose!"

"A good solution," he thought, and fearing that he would change his mind, he quickly put both letters into an envelope and went out.

The sun shone large and bright, white snowflakes circling in the wind. The shops were already closing up. Bender ran quickly to the end of the street toward the post box. He opened the flap, ready to throw the letter in, when suddenly he held himself back. He could hear the flap clapping closed, and he shuddered at the thought that he would even consider doing something so irreversible.

"Even more laughable," he said to himself, wondering why he hadn't realized sooner that sending both letters at once was even worse, far more shameful, pathetic, and disgusting.

A girl walked past, brushing her body against him, and he remembered what he had written about the strong current that flowed through him when Rokhl had taken him by the hand . . . the envelope in his hand was already soaked by the melting snow. He was cold. His feet had started to freeze; in his haste he had forgotten to put on his galoshes. He let go of the post box flap, tore the letters to shreds, and let the wind blow the pieces in every direction. "I don't need it. I don't need anything, I don't need anybody," he mumbled to himself, walking home with quick steps, hunched over.

Bender paced around his room for a long time. Thoughts as heavy as lead trudged through his mind. He wasn't thinking about Rokhl but instead was taking stock of his life. Everything that went through his head, all of his thoughts and deeds, the whole ten years of his wandering, it all seemed like one long chain of pondering and philosophizing and lamenting, like something unnatural that aroused only disgust and scorn.

He wanted to drive the thoughts from his head, but they seemed to cling to his brain, filling up the space like a swarm of flies that cannot be shooed away. The room was full of cigarette smoke. From outside, the white rooftops looked in. The clock struck two. "I need to be in the office tomorrow morning," he thought. He stopped in the middle of the room and looked upward, letting his arms hang limp toward his feet, and he said aloud, clearly and precisely, word by word, like a pupil reciting a lesson:

"And-if-I-want-I-can-be-calm—completely calm . . ."

His shadow on the floor below him aped his every movement, but remained silent.

1907

Gossip

Bernshteyn's dining room was full of guests. There were women of various ages, a young lady of about fifteen or sixteen, two men, and the host himself, Mr. Bernshteyn. The women were engrossed in gossip, while the men played cards. Neither group was entirely at ease.

The women were hindered in their gossiping by the presence of the young lady, a brunette with intense eyes, a gentle face, and lively, impulsive movements. They were obliged to talk over her head in hushed tones, using innuendo and sometimes even skipping over the most interesting, piquant details entirely. The men, who for their part would have been up for a proper game of rummy in five hands, were bored by the game of klaberjass. In the end all eyes turned to Grosman, one of the three card players, a man of about thirty with a short, black beard and a mischievous, sardonic expression. He was not rich, but he was well liked in the rich households of the group's circle. Known for his intelligence and culture, he was good at telling anecdotes and an expert in the latest literary and artistic scandals.

"Pan Grosman will tell us a story," the lady of the house, Mrs. Bernshteyn, said, addressing him in Polish.

Mr. Bernshteyn repeated the suggestion in Russian, and finally the third man among them, a big shot moneylender to princes and generals—and quite wealthy himself—repeated the request in no-nonsense Yiddish: "Come on then, organ-grinder, turn the handle! Out with it!"

Normally Grosman would not need to be asked twice. This time, however, he was reticent. Leaning with his chin in his hand, he turned his curly-haired head toward the girl and stared at her with his cold, cunning eyes until the poor creature felt her face burning and all but burst into tears. Everyone understood that mute scene and smiled: Grosman wanted to recount a saucy anecdote and was letting the girl know that she should leave the room. The girl, however, did not get the hint. Grosman's prolonged stare had left her head reeling, her thoughts twisting and somersaulting like crazed devils. Her vision started to blur and her corset felt tighter; she found it hard to breathe. It was Grosman himself, the Mephistopheles of their little society, who finally took pity on her. "*Fraylin* Róża, would you be so kind as to go out into the drawing room and play a little something on the fortepiano?"

The girl acquiesced, exiting to the accompaniment of muffled laughter. What she did out there, whether she loosened her corset or wept silently, our guests never knew. She certainly didn't play on the fortepiano—not a single note could be heard from the drawing room. The guests, including the girl's aunt, Mrs. Knepfenmakher, were not bothered in the slightest by the scene, which seemed so natural to them and entirely in character for a joker like Pan Grosman.

"Allow me to tell you an anecdote," he began, "about some mutual acquaintances of ours. In fact, they were supposed to be with us tonight, but seeing as they couldn't make it, I think we can allow ourselves to indulge in a little gossip at their expense, no?"

Everyone immediately guessed to whom he was referring: the Fayermans, of course, the richest family in their circle. Mr. Fayerman owned a factory and his own house, and he was known as a crafty fellow who was always involved in some court case or other, never failing to get his way in the end. Mrs. Fayerman lived the high life of the intelligentsia and was always in the process of learning several languages at any given time. She frequently employed governesses and teachers, and she had many connections in the café-based literary artistic market. Mr. Fayerman aroused their jealousy, while they hated Madam Berta Fayerman for her pride. The preamble to the anecdote went down well with the audience.

"Come on, then!" shouted the moneylender.

Grosman continued.

"Things have gone sour between them, you see," he said, switching to Yiddish. "They were on the verge of a divorce. I swear it as you see me here, a divorce! You're surprised? What's surprising is they've managed to stay together for almost fifteen years. Berta has had maybe a dozen lovers; I can name five of them myself. You think Fayerman doesn't know? A cunning fellow like that? Imagine something like this getting past him! No, instead he reasoned to himself: 'You can do what you like, and I'll do what I like; you go ahead and travel out of town with one of your *rascals*'—that's what he calls them—'and don't bother me.' He doesn't let himself be pushed around.

"And they lived happily like that, upon my word. Rumor has it they even bumped into each other once. She was sitting in a booth with her 'rascal' while he was with some crashing bore in the adjacent booth, and they met in the next room—that was it, nothing happened! They held their tongues and continued living their good life together.

"But now suddenly things are bad, there are dramatic scenes, threats of a divorce! What's changed? It's a surprise, to say the least. But believe me, you need to know Fayerman. He is a calm, peaceful man. To Berta he's as soft as butter, kisses her forehead. But one thing he doesn't appreciate is to be pestered. If you stand in his way, then he's capable of anything: a scandal, a divorce! And lately Berta has started to get on his nerves."

The audience listened with rapt attention. In their eyes Grosman had risen to the level of a prophet whose words were always on target, resonating with the deepest parts of their souls, a speaker who could always detect that most compelling, most salient detail. The women were afraid to move for fear of disturbing him. The two men listened, wide-eyed, with an earnestness more appropriate for a thousand-ruble business deal.

He continued: "Lately things have been going badly for Berta. One of her 'rascals,' Shemenski, cast her aside. Guess why! Because she tormented him with the idea of growing a mustache, and just when he wanted to become an actor. Then along came the disturbances, the war situation. As you all know she went abroad, but when she came back," Grosman changed his tone, "Berta was no longer the woman she had been a few years before . . .'"

"She wears makeup!" one of the women said, a little too loudly, unable to restrain herself.

"Please, I ask you not to interrupt," said Grosman calmly, feeling his hold over the audience. "She's worn makeup for two years now. I remember distinctly; it caused her a lot of pain. I give you my word: when she talks about 'the deep tragedy of her soul' I know that the tragedy is nothing more or nothing less than the pain she feels at having to wear makeup. I said as much to Shemenski."

The storyteller paused for a moment to allow for a ripple of subdued laughter. He continued:

"Berta felt very bad. She stayed at home, heartbroken. It cannot be any great joy for a woman to be idle, sitting inside all day, ruminating over and over about the fact that she has grown old and must powder herself. One thing for which I greatly respect my sex, the masculine one, is that we tend not to be as afraid of growing old as women seem to be. On the other hand, women fear death less than we do, and they die much more calmly and with much more decorum."

"Come on then, *katay*, keep going!" urged the moneylender. "Why all this philosophizing? Get to the point!"

Grosman was noticeably offended; he made a sour face but continued, eager to bring the story to its conclusion.

"So Berta started to pester her husband with questions: where was he going, where had he been, what was he doing, and so on. He advised her to concentrate on the children, to which she responded that his spirit was crude and mercenary and that he did not understand her moods. That was the end of their domestic bliss. He went as far as to heap insults on her in public. . . It's so crude, it pains me to talk about it."

They pleaded with Grosman from all sides to continue his story. The women begged with such soft, tender voices and helpless faces, as though they were all in love with Grosman, a strategy that became less tolerable the older the woman.

"Don't stop, keep going! The gentleman will indulge us," one said in Polish. "Do us a favor, be so kind," another called in Russian—they begged him all around.

The host, Mr. Bernshteyn, called out simply in Russian: "You must tell us! How dare you leave us hanging in the middle of a story!"

"Very well, in that case, I'll tell you," said Grosman, allowing himself to be swayed.

"One evening a group was playing cards at Fayerman's house, and Berta was making eyes at a certain Mr. Feldman. You wouldn't know him; he shares a courtyard with the Fayermans. He's a complete socialist; I swear it, a socialist. You should hear him speak! Now Berta, you must understand, has lately grown very fond of socialism. Ever since Shemenski finished with her she doesn't talk about art. Never mind art, the main thing is the class struggle and so on.

"It was the evening of terrible unrest on the streets. The militia had assembled by the gate outside. Everyone was on edge, gathering in groups in their houses. The Fayermans' place was a central gathering point, on account of their telephone. All ears were turned to the streets outside, trying to make out what was happening. *Bang! Bang!* Gunfire in the distance. Berta was pacing restlessly to and fro, nagging her husband, telling him he should stop playing cards. He—you can just picture it—answered calmly: 'You're tired, Berta; go to bed.' He even gave her a kiss on the forehead.

"How could Berta go to bed? The whole day she had been dying of boredom, and now there was a socialist—a handsome, dark-haired young man to boot, with black, burning eyes—sitting right there in her living room. You should have seen him! And outside: a terrible, oppressive mood . . . To cut a long story short, Berta grabbed the cards from the table and ripped them to pieces before falling upon her husband, calling him a bourgeois: how could he indulge in card games when war was cooking in the streets? It was a scandal, a real scandal!

"Fayerman went as red as a flame; he stood up and let her have it, fifteen years' worth of reproaches coming out at once: 'I know what you're up to,' he screamed. 'It's a new lover you want! Shemenski cast you aside. No one will even look at you, you wretched woman! Sit down and be quiet, bite your finger if you want, climb the walls.'

"It was quite a scene.

"It was a stroke of luck that Feldman got involved. If not for him, it would have surely come to a divorce. Upon my word!"

The audience were beside themselves with delight. Grosman described the saucy details of the love between Madam Fayerman and Feldman with cynicism: the romance calmed the warring couple, restoring them to a state of peace.

But the story was cut short by an unexpected event: the phone rang in the lobby, and shortly thereafter the Fayermans entered the room. Mr. Fayerman—a tall, well-built man of about forty with small, crafty eyes, strong, heavy footsteps, and a face that seemed to say: "I can fool anyone, but they can't fool me"—and Mrs. Fayerman, a woman of around thirty-five with light brown hair, shapely eyebrows, and traces of erstwhile beauty. Her face was a curious mixture of apathy and greed. Her subtle makeup was hardly noticeable, and a dull, withered paleness played across her cheeks. A wicked little flame burned in her eyes, and her whole manner seemed the opposite of her husband's: "I've always been fooled, always will be, and I'll let myself be fooled again, because the sin is so sweet."

Their entrance left the whole company quite shaken. Some stood up from their seats; some went pale; others went red. But once Berta had kissed everyone and her husband had greeted them, the tension gradually dissipated and they started chatting and spreading gossip for all they were worth.

The evening, however, was not destined to run smoothly. There was another little scandal yet to come, brought on by the young Miss Róża who had been chased out into next room, and about whom the company had all but forgotten.

The offended girl had been sitting out in the next room the whole time. At first she'd felt bewildered by her rude exile. Lighting the lamp next to the fortepiano, she fell down exhausted onto the chair, only to spring to her feet a moment later. Then she sat down again, trying to compose herself. In the end she burst into tears, the realization that she had been offended building up inside her. Angrily, she put out the light and had a good cry. A little later she lit the lamp again but continued sobbing quietly, resigned.

At length she tired of the whole thing, stood behind the closed door, and listened. Her curiosity to hear what Grosman had to say made her forget the offense and her tears. Pressing her ear against the door, she listened with bated breath, afraid of missing a single word. But then Grosman stopped. Ten minutes passed. Another ten, and still no one called for her. The anger rose up again inside her young heart, and she wept.

Finally unable to hold it in anymore, she opened the door and entered the room. Grosman was the first to meet her gaze. All the shame and hatred seemed to surge inside her, flowing through her entire body. And feeling that she was about to burst into a flood of tears, she lashed out angrily at Grosman:

"You're a fraud!'" she said. "First you say such horrible things about Madam Berta, and now you flatter her! A fraud. Madam Berta! Spit in his face! He's a bad, wicked man. . ."

She couldn't say more than that, her words drowning in tears.

The guests exchanged glances. The women let their heads hang low, with sour expressions; the men glared and furrowed their brows. Madam Berta and her husband stood up and then sat back down again. Silence reigned; the atmosphere became unbearably tense. Róża fled to the kitchen and threw herself down on the chair, crying now in earnest.

It made such a scandal that Grosman had something to talk about, again and again, in many houses for quite some time.

1906

The Golden Fantasy

"You claim that there are people in this world without fantasies, who live without hope or illusions? In my opinion you're quite wrong. I could no more conceive of a human life without oxygen as one without hope."

The young, newly qualified doctor stroked his black goatee and continued.

"If you wish, I'll tell you the story of a man who's currently with us in the psychiatric ward. Five years ago, long before he came here, he was an acquaintance of mine. I had been kicked out of the university and found myself in a circle of very interesting young people: lost, rejected, and adrift. We stuck together as friends bound by the vagaries of life, despite having quite different characters and beliefs.

"Not much is left of our little group now: some took their own lives, one is in Siberia, one died in prison, some have moved on to other careers. But forgive me, I wanted to tell you about the man without illusions who is now in the madhouse. I knew him and I think I understood him well enough, though for the longest time he was something of a puzzle to me. Not just to me in fact; everyone who knew him—Gurshteyn is his name—was taken aback by the extent of his serenity and apathy. Nothing, it seemed, could stir his heart or have any effect on his blank, nonchalantly satisfied face, nor could anything wipe away the smile in those lifeless eyes of his. No event, either in the world at large or in his own circle of acquaintances, ever took him by surprise.

"He had an explanation for everything. All things had some cause, he would say, it made no difference whether we knew about it or not; why then be surprised? Such a philosophy suited his lethargic disposition. It was deeply rooted in his character and he preached it to others at every opportunity.

"Gurshteyn was exceptionally lazy. It wasn't just work or physical effort that he avoided; even the effort of thinking was a burden to him. His usual mantra was that there was an explanation for everything, and whenever you tried to tell him something, he'd say, "I already knew that," with his habitual smile, feeling smug and clever, much more clever than the rest of us young hot-heads with our endless problems. Obviously he was incapable of making a living by himself. The rest of us did what we needed to scrape by. One taught private lessons, another transcribed for a lawyer, another did the accounts in a shop, another had a scholarship to study sculpture at an art school. We seethed and argued; loved and hated; here sad, there happy, all the while plagued by some deep inner dissatisfaction. Only Gurshteyn did nothing, pretending to look for a job while living off money he borrowed from the rest of us. Yet he was calm and contented, without doubts, complaints, or worries. Such rare happiness!

"You couldn't really say that we were fond of him, but he was one of us, lost and rejected by the world. On top of which, he was poor and often went hungry; how then could we ignore him? How could we not lend him some money and treat him as a friend? And yet he remained a stranger to us. It seemed as if no one had ever shaken his hand or given him a friendly pat on the shoulder. It was hard to imagine otherwise. I don't think it bothered him much either. He seemed not to notice it, and even if he did, he would have been too lazy to think about it and would have treated us to more of his own particular brand of philosophizing: 'Certainly there must be some explanation as to why I'm so alien. Whether it lies in my birth or in how I was raised, or in my intellectual development—it all amounts to the same thing.'

"Sometimes we hated him. His apathy and his way of always belittling others and claiming to understand everything would often spill over into cynicism and boorishness. In those moments we had sharp words for him.

"At the time we were all stunned by the deeds of a certain Kaltberg. How intriguing he was! I doubt that I'll meet another like him as long as I live. He was an uncommonly good-hearted man with a profound sympathy for all who suffered, whether close or distant. He understood everyone, right down to the hidden corners of their soul, and he was always ready to help in whatever way he could. Kaltberg became acquainted with a poor, unfortunate girl. She was a hunchback. Her misery touched him deeply; he never ceased to feel for that unfortunate creature, and he announced that he was prepared to marry her. This caused quite a stir. We constantly talked about him, with wonder and passion for such a heroic deed. But just imagine how our Gurshteyn heard the story: indifferently, and with his habitual dismissive wave of the hand.

"'What's the big surprise?' he said. 'He's one of those for whom nothing exists in the world but suffering. That is the scale with which he measures people. One who suffers more than others is more attractive to him. And those who don't suffer don't even exist for him, they amount to a simple zero. I understood it quite well, as he'd long been this way.'

"At that point one of our company could no longer restrain himself and cried out: 'You are a heartless man, that's what you are! You think you understand everything!'

"Taken aback, Gurshteyn tried to shrug it off. But the abrupt words had their effect.

"Our vexed friend was only saying what we were all thinking. From then on, we only needed the slightest pretext to reproach Gurshteyn for his heartlessness.

"'What is a person without a heart?' he asked me once, confidentially, with a tone as if we weren't talking about him but some hypothetical heartless person. 'What is that? A foolish, empty term without meaning, I think. Can I not feel what others feel?'

"But when I tried to debate him, to convince him that 'heartless' was a meaningful term, he was prepared to change his mind.

"'Well, maybe not, maybe I have an intellectual and physical constitution that causes me to not feel as others do. What's wrong with that? Some people are created one way, and others another.'

"And then there was a second case, which showed just how much he lacked fantasy and illusions, as you call it, an event which struck us all with a devastating shock. One of our acquaintances, a young man who was barely nineteen years old—he was studying to be a sculptor and living off his scholarship—hanged himself in his room. They only found him three days later when his face was already black and deformed; he was unrecognizable. He left a short note on the table in which he wrote: 'I am convinced that I will never create a harmonious work of art; without harmony there is no art, and without art there is nothing left for me in life. I have lived surrounded by ugliness, and I die in ugliness. What choice do I have? I do not have the money to buy a revolver, and even if I lived longer I'd probably never be able to afford one. To my friends, and particularly to Kaltberg, I say my final farewell.'

"The incident left a bitter taste in our mouths. We lamented the gruesome loss of our pale, young friend, recalling him with tears in our eyes. A feeling of dread befell us. We felt like the patients in a hospital when one of their number dies. Will not one of us soon follow his lead and come to a similar end? Who will it be? Sadness lay heavy on our hearts. We could not bring ourselves to talk about other things, and to talk about that one doleful thought was too painful. That's when Gurshteyn showed us the full extent of his cold-bloodedness.

"'I am not at all surprised that when one's whole life is tied to one thing that dominates all one's thoughts and feelings, then when that central point suddenly disappears one takes one's own life. It's quite possible, though, that in time he could have created something greater than he'd ever dreamed of. Therein lies the error . . .'

"We hated him for saying those words, and we poured out our entire bitter hearts at him.

"'A heartless man! A monster!'

"He was bombarded with insults from all sides. One of us cursed him: 'How are you not ashamed to talk like that? It's inhuman! Vile! If life means so little to you, then tell us, what do you live for?'

"Gurshteyn smiled foolishly, and a fire sparked in his eyes as he calmly shrugged his shoulders and answered:

"'It's not my problem . . . I'm alive.'

"That's the kind of man he was. Can you imagine someone colder or more austere than that? Sometimes his callousness had its own charm, like the attributes of a curious specimen. We sometimes even felt a sort of respect for his clear, sober intellect, so immune to being led astray. There's a man who doesn't know the bitter taste of disappointment, because he is never fooled, has no 'illusions,' no?

"And yet—how will you believe me?—the man was a fantasist, living in a world of cobwebs, and it was his fantasy that caused him to lose his mind. Unbelievable, you'll say, but you can visit him yourself in the mental ward, and my friend, the head of our department and an experienced psychiatrist, will confirm what I'm telling you. He had fed his spirit with an illusion, a glorious illusion. Underneath the external calm and contentedness he hid a deep desire for happiness, a longing to crawl out of his swampy, impoverished, loathsome existence and enjoy the luxuries of the world. He hoped and waited in silence, never forgetting for a moment that this life was not the real one, that soon his real life would begin. He firmly believed that. He was hoping for the day when he would become rich. It's easy to imagine how this fantasy developed.

"It wasn't a clear hope at first, but it grew steadily along with his hardship and took root deep in his soul. With time the hope took on a distinctive form: he would win the lottery. He roamed for hours through the streets, engrossed in his daydreams, ever more beautiful images swimming before his eyes. He grew in status in his mind's eye. He became wealthy, educated, a fine person, a gentleman. 'What a false impression my friends have of me!' he thought. 'Now they see it, all the good aspects of my character are clear now.' And then . . . women, love, travel under the hot skies of Spain and on the high, snowy mountains of Switzerland. He imagined it all in such vivid detail. It was a sort of intoxication: the more you drink, the more you want. He was loath to interrupt his blissful reveries and so he continued to dream.

"We often stopped him in the street while he was deep in thought. No one knew what it was that absorbed him so much that he always found excuses to get rid of us. Eventually though we discovered his secret; it was pathetic and also sad. Kaltberg, with his deep feeling for humanity, took a greater interest in him, felt such empathy for him that he started to lend him money more often.

"In the end Gurshteyn wanted to try his luck and take part in the lottery jackpot; he came to Kaltberg to borrow a few rubles. Kaltberg asked him what he needed the money for. At first, Gurshteyn was evasive, but in the end he admitted that he intended to play the lottery. Anyone else would have answered him with derision, but Kaltberg, feeling that something was not quite right, explained to him, gently, that it was nonsense; he would never win, and there were people out there starving, in need of a ruble for more important things.

"And so, with his first steps toward realizing his hopes, our fantasist came head on with reality. He was ashamed, in front of Kaltberg, and particularly in front of us. We heard the story from Kaltberg, who never kept secrets. But that did not stop Gurshteyn from daydreaming about the happy times to come. The fantasy soon took prime position in his life. He woke up to it, he went to bed with it, and he wandered the streets with it. It went on like this for quite some time, for years in fact.

"Perhaps he knew he was living in a dream, that his reason had been beaten, but he was no longer capable of renouncing it. Thinking about it was so pleasant, he felt so happy, so free! Why stop?

"Meanwhile, our company spread out far and wide; everyone did what they could. Some of us found work, some of us emigrated, and there was another suicide. The accountant made a career for himself. Gurshteyn remained unchanged, wandering around all alone with his golden fantasy, all the while starving and sinking ever deeper into poverty. And then one day he came to the happy shore: his fantasy became reality. He began counting and recounting paper banknotes: pieces of paper that he had collected on the street.

"You can see him to this day in the hospital," the doctor concluded.

1906

Don't Say a Word!

Felye Faynshteyn kept a vial of potassium cyanide with her at all times. At any moment—if she wanted to—she could swallow the sharp poison in one sip, and a few moments later she would be dead. It all seemed so easy to do, as simple as lying down and drifting off to sleep.

Some years before, around the time that she had last been so horribly betrayed and so deeply insulted, she had decided that enough was enough. She could no longer stand the endless torment. She must—by her own hand—break the chain of suffering that would otherwise continue unbroken for as long as she lived. Her youth was already starting to wither. With each passing day the pain in her heart grew, a yearning that gnawed away inside her and that did not cease even for a minute. She had grown sick of people. The latest incident had opened her eyes to what men really desired from her. She felt like a helpless creature pursued by hunters through the woods. Deep down her heart yearned for them, yet in her thoughts she hated them so much.

One night she took the vial out of her bag, set it down onto the stool next to her desk, and wrote two short letters, one to her mother and the other to her younger sister. She got undressed and put on clean underwear. Then she covered the cushions with white pillowcases and changed the sheets so that her bed shone white and new. She stood in front of the mirror in a clean shirt and unbraided her black hair—the most beautiful thing that she had left—letting it fall freely over her shoulders. With calm, quiet steps she approached the bed and lay down. She was in no hurry. She had decided to die peacefully and beautifully, neither in haste nor in a moment of panic. She was a proud woman with deep self-respect, unable to entertain a single doubt that she would be able to abide by her decision.

She stretched her slim body out on the bed—her arms spread limply on the blanket—closed her eyes, and let her mind wander. The thought of her imminent death did not frighten her. She did not want to think about those few minutes between drinking the poison and the end. It was foolish to be afraid! Two, three minutes of pain—and nothing more. Afterward . . . afterward her body would stiffen in the bed, eyes closed, her heart no longer beating, her brain filled with lead, not a trace of anguish to be seen. Even now she rejoiced in the idea that her heart would be free from those feelings choking it day and night. Her otherwise earnest expression revealed the faintest hint of a smile.

Opening her eyes, she brushed the hair from her face and reached out toward the stool. The light, the table, the chair, and all the other things in her room struck her eyes in a new way. She took pleasure in looking at them, as though she had never seen them before. Everything—from the stool to the stitched hem of the shirt on her breast to her own calmly outstretched arms—seemed so unfamiliar and yet familiar, so new and yet so old. A colorful brightness that seemed to grow from her own being poured out over everything, giving an entirely new tone to the world, her own being, and all her thoughts and feelings. The world was now still, calm, and safe.

"Now I will die," she thought. And even that thought, which she had been carrying around with her for so long, seemed new. Within that very thought lay a blessed calmness that she could not have conceived of before. The vial was already at her lips. As she sat up to drink, a new idea came to her in a flash, an idea that seemed unfathomable and all-encompassing, like the secret of life and death itself. She stopped—still holding the vial to her mouth—to reflect on the enormity of this new thought. She had no words to describe it, and yet it was all so clear and simple. That world of yearning and anguish, pain and torment was already behind her, and a new world had opened itself up to her, a world where pain was impossible, where there was nothing more to fear, a world without yearning or desire, a peaceful and protected world. Right at that very moment she felt as if she was standing on the border between life and death, right where they intersected, where they swallowed each other up and became one.

She closed her eyes once more and leaned back onto the pillow. Familiar faces appeared before her eyes, shimmering like flecks of light on a shadowy background. She could see the smiling, tender, and yet so hated face of the student who had most recently broken her heart. She no longer felt any animosity toward him, no rancor. His face was calm and sanctified, like her new frame of mind, like the whole world. Other faces floated by: her mother, her sister, acquaintances—and they all wore the same expression.

"Am I already dead?" she asked herself. But she was not dead; the vial of poison was still in her hand, she was still holding it to her lips. And in the mystical lucidity of her mind a clear idea took shape: "I am dying calmly, happily, and with joy." Soon a second thought took shape beside the first: "If one can die so peacefully and happily, what is there to be afraid of in life? What's the rush?"

The whole night she lay with her eyes closed, her mind filling up with murky images and ideas. When she awoke and opened her eyes the next morning, the glow of the previous night still shone brightly. Not a shadow of longing was left.

"Did I lack the courage to follow through?" she asked herself that day. "But, no! I can die peacefully whenever the anguish starts again in my heart. I will do it, and without a trembling hand, having reflected with a clear mind." So she kept the vial of poison, ready to use it should she ever need to.

She continued her life for the time being, with the feeling that she was on the threshold of death. That night had left its mark. Her demeanor, facial expressions, mannerisms, and even her voice had all changed. She radiated a deep, incomprehensible earnestness and gravity. People moved gently and spoke quietly in her presence. Those who laughed were shocked by the volume of their own voices. People felt a newfound respect for her; their eyes were drawn toward her, to her fine hands with the long white fingers, as if by some magnetic force. She continued to give lessons and manage her household finances. She spoke plainly and to the point, but her simple words about everyday, domestic matters made a strange impression, as if some larger secret lay hidden beneath them. She had become a stranger in her own home. Neither her sick mother nor her sister spoke with her more than was necessary. It was clear to all that she carried her unhappiness hidden deep in her heart.

Days turned into weeks, and she lived silently, in a fog. Her mother died and her sister finished school. She herself was older now, but it seemed as if nothing had changed. Everything had happened so naturally and logically that she felt as though it could not have been otherwise. On that fateful day everything had been set, and since then nothing had budged. Even her youth had stopped fading, and she remained the same as she had been the year before, the same as two years before. She lived without joy and without suffering, day in and day out experiencing the same apathy. Sometimes it seemed as if she had lost the ability to differentiate between pain and joy, between happiness and unhappiness. With time she developed a certain taste. She no longer liked colorful clothes, always wearing either black or—when she was at home—white. Her blouses were so cleverly tailored that they did not reveal anything of her breasts, and she had no tolerance for novels or love poetry; both seemed so repulsive to her, as if someone were manhandling a sacred relic with shameless, ungainly hands.

Her younger sister, Anna, had grown up to be gifted and beautiful. Men liked her, and as she started falling in love she discovered the same disturbed feelings that Felye had known so well. Anna took to coming home late at night, sometimes happy, sometimes sad, often crying. Felye observed her through sad, passive eyes and could feel the young, fresh life of her sister tearing itself apart, like her own had done, but she didn't say a word. She said nothing because she had nothing to say. Once in a while she would sit stroking her sister's hair and ask how late it was. Her younger sister would then nestle up to her, crying softly, her young body trembling under Felye's hand. Felye would stand up, her heart becoming uneasy, something beginning to gnaw inside her. She remembered the vial.

She would asked herself in such moments of agitation if the time had come. But the mere thought of it was enough to calm her heart, everything becoming comprehensible and natural, and sometimes the frontier between pain and joy would disappear.

Each day, the tenants of the summer houses by Amarlo who had gathered in the evening by the train station would be confronted with a female figure whom they could not avoid staring at. She was thin, with a pale face. She was no longer young, but she held herself with pride. She walked slowly, her arms hanging straight by her sides. Her downcast eyelids occasionally rose to reveal eyes—absent yet sharp—that spoke a language no one understood. It was Felye. She felt the curious stares on all sides, heard how they mumbled things about her, and was annoyed that she had let her sister convince her to come out to stay at a guest house.

"To what end?" she thought, agitated.

Everything repulsed her: the young lives swarming around her, the endless flirting, the happy laughter, the running and singing, the gangs of young people with whom even her sister spent time—she was repulsed by it, and she sank even deeper into her habitual musing about death. In those moments she sometimes looked around with pride: pride in her own stifled heart and in the suffering that she did not share with anyone. She was proud of her maidenhood, which she had kept like a holy, withered flower, but she could no longer stand the mild evenings, the red sunsets, the play of colors on the western sky, or the slow descent of darkness. They stirred her heart too much, waking the old forgotten yearnings, and as she walked home her thoughts constantly turned to the vial.

On one such evening she came home to find her sister in tears. She was sitting on the bed, her arms wrapped around the headrest. At Felye's approach, her sister buried her face in her hands. The gesture reminded Felye of her own experiences of coming home insulted, her heart unable to stand those terrible, bitter feelings. Back then, she had sat in exactly the same way, dwelling on the pain and crying for hours.

"Look how she is tormented right now!" she thought, and for the first time it occurred to Felye that she must comfort her sister. She sat down beside her and began to stroke her hair.

"Don't cry, Anna, don't cry . . ."

Her little sister only sobbed all the more, her shoulders shaking. Suddenly she turned around to Felye and nuzzled up to her, holding her head against Felye's chest.

"I can't take it anymore," she said in an impulsive tone. "I can't. I'd rather die, I don't want to live like this."

"I understand, child," Felye said quietly, "I understand everything. I have gone through all of that myself, for many years, for so many years, and you see—I'm still alive . . ."

She fell silent, shocked by how unstable her own words sounded. And Anna, who had never heard her sister talk in such a tone, looked up at her with curiosity, her eyes silently begging Felye to continue.

"You have no idea, sister, what a person can suffer through in this world, what it means to love and be betrayed and insulted. The first time I fell in love, I was so happy. I didn't think that I could stand it. And the second time, my happiness was already mixed with bitterness. The third time, I wept and pined, pined and wept. The fourth time was even worse, always worse and worse."

She stopped, humiliated by her own words. She hugged her sister, who quietly pleaded: "Don't stop, tell me. Tell me everything."

Felye wanted to tell her the final story, which seemed so important to her, so terrible and brutal. But she froze at the first words.

"No, no . . . I won't tell you. You wouldn't understand."

But Anna stood up next to her and pleaded.

"Tell me, please, I understand everything. The devil only knows what they think of us . . ."

Those words hurt Felye deeply. She wanted to convince her sister that she was wrong, that her own unhappiness had been different, that she had even loved differently, so she continued her story, but the more she told, the more insignificant it all seemed. It was like sinking into quicksand: the more you struggle to escape, the deeper you sink.

"It wasn't like that, you understand. We had gone for a walk, afterward he accompanied me home. We were riding in a carriage and suddenly he took me in his arms and kissed me, I was terrified . . ."

But as she spoke she thought, "This is stupid, banal. This is not what I want to say."

Her heart emptied; she felt drained and broken. Suddenly a wild and violent pain pressed against her chest. Her eyes, which had not seen a tear in so many years, were suddenly wet, and she cried in front of her sister. She cried long and bitterly, but far from bringing her relief the tears lay like heavy stones on her heart.

The next morning Anna awoke to find her sister dead—the vial had been emptied—and on the table lay a note, containing the following words:

"I am dying, sister. Actually, I died a long time ago. Take care of yourself. If it is your fate to suffer as much as I have suffered, do not share your pain with anyone. Keep it safe in your own heart, so that it remains hidden and holy. Above all don't say anything to anyone, my sister. Whatever you do, don't say a word!"

1907

Notes

Fliglman

Fliglman:
The name literally means "wing-man," perhaps an allusion to his uprooted nature, a man with his head in the clouds. As is sometimes the case with Nomberg's characters, we only learn his surname.

Shammes:
See glossary.

Buddha, Spinoza, Kant:
Baruch Spinoza (1632–1677): Dutch philosopher of Jewish descent. Immanuel Kant (1724–1804): German philosopher, one of the central figures in modern philosophy. Buddha: by the 18th century western philosophers, such as Schopenhauer and Nietzsche, began to take great interest in Buddhist teachings. Nomberg himself makes frequent allusions to Buddha in his writings.

Kuniv:
Possibly Kuniv in Volhynia, modern Ukraine, described as a shabby little town on a muddy plain with half a dozen shops in the market square, around which the Jewish inhabitants lived.

Weltanschauung:
(Lit: world view) A concept fundamental to German philosophy, referring to the framework of ideas and beliefs forming a global description

through which an individual or group observes, interprets, and interacts with the world. Fliglman, perhaps taking the concept too literally, is preoccupied with cultivating his own Weltanschauung.

Fifth floor:
The higher buildings in Warsaw at the time were five or six stories high. Fliglman probably lives on the top floor in a garret-style apartment.

Levantkovski:
The name has echoes of the Levant.

Levantkovski's poem:
The quotation from Levantkovski's poem, in Hebrew in the original, is a simple rhyming couplet. *"Ma yofe hateve, al kol har vegeve"* (lit. "How beautiful is nature, every hill and every mountain").

Schopenhauer:
Arthur Schopenhauer (1788–1860) German philosopher whose system of aesthetics, metaphysics, and ethics was an example of philosophical pessimism. His posthumous influence, particularly in the fields of literature and music, was considerable.

The Vistula:
(Yiddish: *Vaysl*) The largest river in Poland, which runs through Warsaw separating the city center on the left bank from the suburb of Praga on the right bank.

The bridge over the Vistula:
The Kierbedź Bridge (officially known as the Alexander Bridge before Polish independence). Opened in 1864, it was the first steel truss bridge over the Vistula and one of the most modern bridges in Europe. Built for road traffic, it had tracks for horse-drawn trams. There were pedestrian walkways on either side, separated from the road traffic.

A fiery L shape:
In the original: "a fiery *daled*," referring to the shape of the Hebrew letter *daled*, roughly similar to an upside-down L.

Higher Education

Title in Yiddish: "*a kursistke*" (lit: a female student).

Wonderful person:
In Russian in the original: *"Khoroshi chudni chelovek."*

The South of Russia:
Imprecise geographical term usually denoting the southern parts of European Imperial Russia, including the north Caucasus and Ukraine.

Fidler:
Surname meaning "fiddler." Another of the many Nomberg characters whose name begins with the Hebrew letter *fey.*

Zemstvo:
Local organs of self-government, with some degree of freedom from centralized bureaucratic control, responsible for various activities such as charity, local education, health services, road building, etc. Zemstvos employed technical experts such as teachers, doctors, engineers, statisticians, etc.—many of whom had liberal or social democratic political leanings—referred to collectively as the "Third Element."

Batistini:
Mattia Batistini (1856–1928), known as "king of the baritones," was an Italian opera singer who was particularly successful throughout Eastern Europe.

Kovno:
Modern-day Kaunas, Lithuania.

Dobry wieczór:
Polish: Good evening.

A four:
In the Russian five-point grading system a four is "good."

Sehr Geehrte:
Formal German salutation (lit: most honored/venerated).

Marzsałkowska Street:
Marszałkowska Street had existed since the 18th century, but by the end of the 19th century it had been extended into a long boulevard and was the bourgeois epicenter of Warsaw, lined with mansions and expensive shops.

Who Is to Blame?

Copied Russian lessons:
Original: "Hectographed Russian lessons." Hectography was a printing process using special ink on a gelatin surface. A cheap and widely used method of copying documents, it was often used for newsletters, amateur magazines, and classroom handouts. Also known as a Jellygraph.

Spasibo:
Russian: Thank you.

Vi kharoshi gospodin:
(Lit: you are a good sir) Finkelman's Russian here is somewhat stilted and obsequious.

Gnädiger Herr:
Formal German salutation (lit: gracious sir).

Crime and Punishment:
The story contains numerous allusions to Fyodor Dostoevsky's *Crime and Punishment*, published in 1866.

Russian calendar/Jewish:
The Russian civil calendar at the time was the Julian calendar, which
has 365 days in a year, whereas the Jewish calendar usually has 353–355
days in a year. Therefore if Finkelman is being paid on a monthly basis
according to the Russian civil calendar he will sometimes have to wait
longer for his wages.

Message-reply card:
A type of postal card where postage was prepaid both ways to facilitate
a prompt reply.

Tore a patch from each of our garments:
Krie, or Keriah: the custom of tearing clothes as a sign of mourning for
a close relative.

Omeyn shelo:
(Amen/may it be so) Formula used in letters.

Lomzhe:
Polish: Łomża, a city in northeastern Poland, home to the Lomzhe
Yeshiva, founded in 1883 in the style of Lithuanian yeshivas.

In a Hasidic House

"Enlightenment":
Referring here to the ideas of the Haskalah *(haskole)* or Jewish enlightenment.

Warsaw accent:
See glossary entry for Litvak.

"I've no tiiiime!":
In Yiddish: *"Kh'o-nish-k'tsaaat!"* Here and throughout Nomberg uses eye
dialect spelling to represent the Hasid's accent. Interesting, in this case,
as the story is told from a Litvak's perspective, and the accent being
ridiculed is Nomberg's own.

Wig:
Married Hasidic women cover their hair with a wig known as a *sheytl.*

Litvak:
See glossary.

Some Hasidic custom:
This is indeed a custom, known as *Negiye* (lit: contact), whereby some orthodox Jews try to avoid physical contact with members of the opposite sex, outside of immediate family members.

Neighbors

A Jew in modern dress:
Yid: *"a daytsh"* (lit: a German).

Grokhovtse:
Pol: Grochowce, small village in southern Poland.

Five thousand rubles:
An astronomical sum at the time, representing several decades worth of wages for an unskilled worker.

. . . he was a cunning heretic:
In the original: he had "a cross in his head." See glossary entry for Litvak.

Itshe-Mayer:
See glossary.

Bareheaded and fully dressed:
The implication being that the Litvak had been outside without a hat, something his Orthodox neighbor couldn't help noticing.

Nighttime blessing:
Hamapl: blessing said before going to bed. The original cites the lines: "who casts the bonds of sleep upon mine eyes . . ."

Straight to the rebbe with an offering:
The Litvak is referring to a *Pidyen,* the traditional offering of money to a Hasidic Rebbe.

"Pour out thy wrath upon the nations . . ."
Line near the end of the Haggadah, from Jeremiah 10:25.

Lunar:
The Litvak uses the German-origin, *daytshmerish* word *mond,* which he figures a Hasid, unfamiliar with vocabulary used only in secular journalistic or scientific writing, would not understand. In the following sentence he uses *"levone,"* the usual Yiddish word for "moon."

Roommates

The surnames Fayner and Gutman have similar etymologies: "fine man" and "good man" respectively.

Dzika Street/Prison/cemetery:
Dzika Street, the Jewish cemetery, and the prison were all located at the northwestern edge of the city; the area beyond was still fields at the time.

Go on then, my friend:
At this point in the original, Fayner says, *"Mir veln zayn af du,"* inviting Gutman to switch from the formal pronoun *ir* to the informal *du.*

Two French socialists:
A reference to Alexandre Millerand and Pierre Baudin, who accepted posts in Pierre Waldeck-Rousseau's "bourgeois" coalition in 1899. It was the first time that socialists had taken up ministerial positions in the French government and gave rise to a heated polemic in leftist circles.

Letters

Bender:
Presumably the same Yankev Bender from "The Game of Love," a few years older now.

Gossip

Mephistopheles:
Name of the demon in the Faust legend.

Rummy . . . klaberjass:
"*Oke*": a variant of rummy, in which players try to form sequences or sets of cards (or tiles).
"*Klaberyash*" (Klaberjass): a trick-taking card game (similar to pinochle).

Katay!:
Russian (archaic) roughly: "Giddy up!" (when addressing a horse).

"Rascals":
Yid: "*shnekes*" (lit: snail): urchin, scamp.

Don't Say a Word!

Original title: "*Shvayg shvester!*" (lit: "Hush, sister!").

Faynshteyn:
Surname meaning "precious stone."

Potassium cyanide:
Colorless crystalline salt, highly soluble in water. Its extreme toxicity in low doses makes it a perennial favorite for poisoners and suicides. Nomberg uses the Russian term word *tsianistii kalii*.

Glossary

agunah (*agune*):
(Lit: anchored or chained woman) A woman whose husband is missing, or who has been abandoned by her husband. Unable to get a divorce, she is therefore "chained" to her marriage and cannot remarry without proof of her husband's death. The status of *agune* was highly undesirable, and the inability to remarry often had dire economic consequences; therefore, the threat of leaving someone as an *agune* could be—and was—used as blackmail by vengeful husbands.

groschen (*groshn*):
Used colloquially to refer to a low value coin, regardless of the currency in question (cf. *penny*).

gymnazium:
In central and Eastern Europe, a secondary school generally preparing students to go on to university.

Haggadah (*hagode*):
Text read during the Passover Seder recounting the story of the liberation of the Jews of Egypt as told in the book of Exodus.

Hasidism/Hasid (*khasidizm* or *khsides, khosid*):
A branch of Orthodox Judaism originating in the 18th century that rapidly gained popularity throughout Eastern Europe. The opponents of Hasidism were known as the misnagdim. The central characteristics of Hasidism include allegiance to a particular rebbe, or spiritual leader,

emphasis on individual prayer, and joyous worship involving singing, and dancing.

Itshe-Mayer:
Derogatory term for a Polish/Hasidic Jew. Itshe-Mayer had been an extremely popular boys' name among Hasidim since the death of the first Gerer Rebbe, Itshe Mayer (Yitzchak Meir) Alter (1799–1866). From a Litvak's point of view, all Hasidim seemed to be called Itshe-Mayer (see also Litvak).

kosher:
In keeping with Jewish law; by extension pure, virtuous, legitimate.

Litvak:
Literally means "Lithuanian Jew" but refers to a group whose regional identity was considerably older and more stable than the borders of Eastern Europe, living in the area roughly equivalent to modern-day Lithuania, Latvia, Belarus, and parts of northeast Poland. The Litvaks differed from the *Poylish* (Polish) Jews and *Galitsyaner* (Galician/Ukrainian) Jews in their dialect, cuisine, temperament, and religious practices.

Stereotypically the Litvaks are cold and rational while the *Poylish/Galitsyaner* Jews are emotional, superstitious, and more strongly influenced by Hasidism.

To the Warsaw Jew, the Litvak's accent sounds clipped and formal, with unusual sibilants often caricatured as a lisp. The long vowels of the Warsaw Jew's speech are perceived by the Litvak as a comical drawl.

A common derogatory term for Livak was *tseylem kop* (lit: crucifix head), referring to the popular folk image that inside the head of every Litvak there was a tiny cross, implying a slippery slope from the Litvak's logic and reason to heresy and apostasy.

Pan/Panie/Pani/Panna:
Polish honorifics were widely used in Yiddish. Pan (lit: sir) is the equivalent of "Mr." (Panie, the vocative form, is used when addressing a man directly). Pani is the equivalent of "Mrs.," while Panna, largely outdated

in modern Polish, was the equivalent of "Miss."

In Polish, Pan/Pani, etc. are also used (along with the verb in the third person) as the formal "you" (cf. "Would sir like a cup of tea?"). In Nomberg's stories, the use of this formal third person is often a cue to the reader that the characters are speaking in Polish.

Reb:
Yiddish honorific, equivalent to "Mr." Used with full name or first name only.

Rebbe:
In Hasidism, the spiritual leader of a Hasidic dynasty; word used by heder/yeshiva students to address their teacher. More generally, a mentor or spiritual guide.

seder (*seyder*):
Holiday meal to mark Passover, celebrated as a family. The meal involves the eating of matzah, ritual foods, and the reading of the Haggadah. Men who had migrated to large cities for work, leaving their families behind in the villages, would often take pains to come home for the Passover seder.

shammes (*shames*; plural *shammosim*):
The caretaker of a synagogue. Often translated as "beadle" or "sexton."

shofar (*shoyfer*):
Ancient musical instrument made from a ram's horn. The shofar is blown during synagogue services on Rosh Hashanah (*rosheshone*) and at the end of Yom Kippur (*yom kiper*). It is also blown every weekday morning during the month of Elul (*elel*) preceding Rosh Hashanah.

Shavuos (*shvues*):
Shavuot, Pentecost, or the Festival of Weeks is a festival marking the wheat harvest in the Land of Israel and celebrating the day Moses received the Torah. Usually falls in early June according to the civil calendar.

tallis *(tales):*
Or tallit, a fringed prayer shawl worn during morning prayer.

tefillin *(tfilin):*
Small leather boxes, sometimes called *phylacteries*, containing tiny scrolls of parchment, that are worn during morning prayer on the forehead and arm, secured by leather straps.

yeshiva *(yeshive):*
School focused on the study of religious texts, particularly the Talmud and Torah. Yeshiva students were adolescent boys who had shown enough intellectual promise to warrant further study. Yeshivas were usually boarding schools, with students often having to leave home and travel some distance to study there. Meals for poorer students were often provided on a charitable basis by nearby families, whereby students could eat at a different house each day of the week, a practice known as *esn teg* (lit. "eating days").

Translator's Acknowledgments

Responsibility for any errors is entirely my own; however, the following people are guilty of encouraging me in various ways.

Thanks to Yitskhok Niborski, who introduced me to Nomberg's story "Fliglman" and patiently answered my litany of questions emailed at ungodly hours of the night. Thanks also to those I accosted with questions in the hallways of the Paris Yiddish Center—Medem Library, particularly Batia Baum and Natalia Krynicka.

Thanks to all those involved with the 2015 Yiddish Book Center Translation Fellowship, particularly organizer Seb Schulman; workshop leaders Katie Silver and Sean Cotter; *khevruse* partners Adrian Silver and Jordan Finkin; and fellowship mentor Lazer Lederhendler for his expertise, encouragement, and generosity.

Thanks also to Eitan Kensky and Yankl Salant for editorial feedback on individual stories and to my unpaid proofreaders, Ellen Kennedy, Olivia Lasky, and Fleur Kuhn-Kennedy. Thanks to Veronica Esposito, Lisa Newman, Mindl Cohen, and all those involved in the book's production.

This translation is dedicated to my family and ambulatory home: Fleur and Samuel.

Daniel Kennedy
Rennes, July 2017

About the Yiddish Book Center

The Yiddish Book Center is a nonprofit organization working to recover, celebrate, and regenerate Yiddish and modern Jewish literature and culture.

The million books recovered by the Yiddish Book Center represent Jews' first sustained literary and cultural encounter with the modern world. The books are a window on the past thousand years of Jewish history, a precursor to modern Jewish writing in English, Hebrew, and other languages, and a springboard for new creativity. Since its founding in 1980, the Center has launched a wide range of bibliographic, educational, and cultural programs to share these treasures with the wider world.

The Yiddish Book Center's Translation Initiative

The tens of thousands of books published in Yiddish contain untold treasures of literature, scholarship, memoir, and other unique documents that tell a rich and complex story of Jewish life in the modern world. Making these works accessible to English readers has become one of our highest priorities, which is why the Center launched a multipronged translation initiative:

- Our Translation Fellowship Program is training and mentoring a new generation of Yiddish literary translators.
- We publish newly translated works in our magazine, *Pakn Treger,* including an annual digital translation issue.
- We post new works in translation every month on yiddishbookcenter.org.
- White Goat Press publishes new translations from Yiddish. Recent titles include *Seeds in the Desert* by Mendel Mann, translated by Heather Valencia.

Recently Published by Yiddish Book Center Translation Fellows

On the Landing: Stories by Yenta Mash, translated by Ellen Cassedy (Northern Illinois University Press/A Yiddish Book Center Translation, 2018)

Oedipus in Brooklyn by Blume Lempel, translated by Ellen Cassedy and Yermiyahu Ahron Taub (Mandel Vilar Press and Dryad Press, 2016)

The People of Godlbozhits by Leyb Rashkin, translated by Jordan Finkin (Syracuse, 2017)

A Death: Notes of a Suicide by Zalman Shneour, translated by Daniel Kennedy (Wakefield Press, 2019)

Diary of a Lonely Girl by Miriam Karpilove, translated by Jessica Kirzane (Syracuse University Press, 2019)

Vilna, My Vilna, by Abraham Karpinowitz, translated by Helen Mintz (Syracuse University Press, 2016)

Judgment, by David Bergelson, translated by Harriet Murav and Sasha Senderovich (Northwestern/A Yiddish Book Center Translation, 2017)

Attractive Hebrews: The Lambert Yiddish Cylinders 1901–1905, translated by Henry Sapoznik (Archeophone Records, 2016)

Pioneers: The First Breach, by S. Ansky, translated by Rose Waldman (Syracuse/A Yiddish Book Center Translation, 2017)

To learn more, visit yiddishbookcenter.org/in-translation

Author and Translator

Hersh Dovid Nomberg (1876–1927) was a writer, essayist and political activist, born in Mszczonów near Warsaw. Raised in a strictly Hasidic environment, Nomberg began to dabble in forbidden secular texts (Russian and German literary texts in particular), whereupon he experienced a crisis of faith. Nomberg's newfound atheism and growing literary ambitions led him to Warsaw where he became a protegé of I. L. Peretz.

He began publishing poems and short stories around 1900 in both Yiddish and Hebrew and was considered one of the most influential Yiddish writers of his generation. Having penned dozens of successful short stories, he shifted his focus toward journalism and politics following the First World War. He was one of the founders of the *Folkspartey*, a party dedicated to safeguarding secular Jewish cultural autonomy within the Polish Republic, for whom he served as a delegate to the *Sejm* in 1919–1920. Though based in Warsaw, Nomberg never stayed in any one place for long. He traveled extensively throughout Western Europe, South America, Russia, and Palestine. He died at the age of fifty-one, having suffered from chronic lung problems for most of his life.

Daniel Kennedy is a literary translator based in France. He is a two-time Yiddish Book Center Translation Fellow, managing editor for translations at *In geveb: a Journal of Yiddish Studies*, and co-founder of Farlag Press.